Henry Collins

The Cistercian Fathers

Lives And Legends Of Certain Saints And Blessed Of The Order Of Citeaux

Henry Collins

The Cistercian Fathers
Lives And Legends Of Certain Saints And Blessed Of The Order Of Citeaux

ISBN/EAN: 9783337391799

Printed in Europe, USA, Canada, Australia, Japan

Cover: Foto ©Andreas Hilbeck / pixelio.de

More available books at **www.hansebooks.com**

THE
CISTERCIAN FATHERS:

OR,

LIVES AND LEGENDS

OF CERTAIN

SAINTS AND BLESSED

OF THE

ORDER OF CITEAUX.

TRANSLATED BY

HENRY COLLINS.

WITH A PREFACE BY THE

REV. W. R. BROWNLOW, M.A.,

AUTHOR OF "ROMA SOTTERRANEA."

FIRST SERIES.

LONDON:
THOMAS RICHARDSON AND SON;
DUBLIN AND DERBY.
NEW YORK: HENRY H. RICHARDSON AND CO.
MDCCCLXXII.

ADVERTISEMENT.

The Cistercian Order has about sixty Canonised Saints. The particulars of their lives are in many cases lost, or are not interesting, or are already published. Besides the Canonised Saints, she has a multitude of holy persons in her catalogue of Blessed. The Lives published in this volume are mostly of this latter class, and are those commemorated in the first six months of her Menology, or Calendar.

CONTENTS.

———

THE Annals of the Cistercian Order abound in Legends, that is, in histories which partake largely of the supernatural character, and in which departed saints, and angels, and devils, play as important and circumstantial a part as men and women of this sublunary world. It may, therefore, be well to say a few words upon the amount of credence which is due to such legends. As a general rule, they are never matters of faith, in the sense in which the miraculous occurrences narrated in Holy Scripture are; but the amount of credence due to each legend varies according to the evidence or authority on which its historical certainty rests. Some have been placed beyond all reasonable doubt, by the formal examination and decision of the Church, while others are hardly within the range of probability.

It must not, however, be supposed that a legend is the same thing as a fable, a myth, or a parable. Mr. Baring-Gould appears to have fallen into this mistake in his "Curious Myths of the Middle Ages," where he puts the Legend of S. Ursula in the same category with the fable of Pope Joan, and the Man in the Moon. The consequence of this confusion is, that to the majority of readers the word "Legend" conveys the idea of something histori-cally untrue. A few words on the dis-tinction between the fable, the parable, the myth, and the legend, may serve to remove misconceptions.

A *fable* is generally intended to convey some lesson in morality. The story itself is often palpably destitute of any pre-tensions to historical fact. The circum-stances related are not only improbable, but impossible. Animals, and trees, and even stones, are represented as holding conversations. These incredible circum-stances are, however, useful in arresting the attention, and conveying the moral lesson intended to be put forth.

A *parable*, as the word is generally understood by Christians, differs from a fable mainly in this, that the truths it is intended to convey are not merely moral, but connected with what is divine. Thus, we should call the story told to David by the woman of Thecua, (2 Kings, xiv.), a fable; while the story told by Nathan to the same king, (2 Kings, xii.), is a parable; although both stories were alike destitute of historical foundation. Here is an instance of the fable and parable approximating each other, so as only to be distinguished by their scope. The parable, however, in the sense in which we have used the word, never passes beyond the limits of the possible. The things of the kingdom of God are symbolized, not by unreal impossibilities, but by their analogy to certain things which do actually take place on earth.

The *myth* differs widely from both the parable and the fable. It professes to be an historical narrative, and, in many cases, has probably some foundation in fact. Its circumstantial details are, however, mere inventions, and are, so to speak, the crystallizations of ideas held in solution by the popular mind. Men naturally prefer the concrete to the abstract, and love to have a distinct person or story in which they may see their ideas embodied. The celebrated "Donation of Constantine" was a myth of this nature. Men knew that, some how or other, it had come to pass that the Pope and Christian Rome had taken the place of the old imperial Rome and the emperor. Constantine had certainly made donations to the Holy Roman Church. The popular mind saw in the supposed "Donations" an explanation of what it knew had actually come to pass, and whoever was the individual author of the fictitious document, which contained the Donations, the popular imagination was the inventor of the myth. The fears and hopes of men, the craving after the marvellous, and many other passions of the human heart, invest the unknown with a character as far from real, as is the ideal character, with which a romantic girl invests the common-place individual with whom she falls in love, from being a true description of the man. By a process similar to what is termed in Mathematics, "integrating differentials," the abstract idea may be discovered from the concrete myth. Thus the Neo-Platonists explained the Greek and Roman mythology, and thus Mr. Furgusson has elaborately explained the Buddhist myths, represented on ancient Indian sculptures. It is, however, easy to fall into dangerous excesses in such explanations, and the ingenious writer on the "Myths of the Middle Ages," above mentioned, has hardly escaped them, while Dean Stanley has been accused, with some justice, of dealing in a similar spirit with some of the historical narratives of Holy Scripture.

The *legend* is to the myth what the parable is to the fable. Like the myth, it claims to be history. If it be not history in each particular case, it has something historical for its ground-work, or it clothes in historical garb the beliefs of men. It makes of abstract doctrines concrete facts.

Properly speaking, the legend is confined to Christianity. The word *legenda* signifies, primarily, the short accounts of the saints read in the Matins of the Divine Office. It afterwards embraced those chronicles of the various Religious orders which were considered edifying reading, and thus we find it defined in Craig's Universal Dictionary: "a chronicle or register of the lives of the Saints, formally read at matins, and at the refectories of Religious Houses." The famous *Legenda Aurea*, was a collection of these stories by the Domicican B. James de Voragine, Archbishop of Genoa, who died in 1292. It was so called by his admirers; for, as Wynkin de Worde says, "Like as passeth gold in value all other metals, so this Legend exceedeth all other books." Longfellow's well known poem is not derived from this source, although the utterly improbable story on which it is founded is a very ancient one, "being," as the poet tells us, "told, and perhaps invented, by Hart-

mann von der Aue, a Minnesinger of the
twelfth century." But, though the term,
"legend," is thus of Christian origin, and,
strictly speaking, implies that the narratives
it contains are Christian, it must be confessed that the term has been, especially of
late years, so widened and lowered in its
signification, as to embrace all the wild,
fabulous, mythological traditions of Greek,
Roman, Indian, and Scandinavian gods and
goddesses. The misfortune of this is, that
when the word is used in its Christian and
primary sense, the reader is apt to conclude
that the narrative spoken of as a legend is
necessarily something untrue; whereas,
many legends are simple narrations of
actual facts. The Christian legend, however, is not necessarily true, although it is
necessarily harmless, and calculated to
convey true ideas. Thus, Longfellow says
of the story on which his Golden Legend
is founded: " It exhibits the virtue of dis-
interestedness and self-sacrifice, and the
power of Faith, Hope, and Charity, sufficient for all the exigencies of life and
death." And this, although the story

itself is evidently untrue, and it would be absolutely wicked for any one to do literally that which is done by the heroine of the story.

As legends are narratives, more or less founded on history, of the sayings and doings of Saints and saintly powers, the supernatural, or the marvellous, enters largely into their composition. To a Catholic reader, this is just what was to be expected, and he is no more surprised at reading of mediæval Saints working miracles, and casting out devils, than he is when he finds similar wonderful works related by the Evangelists of our Lord and the Apostles. A Protestant, who has got a fixed idea that miracles ceased with the apostles, feels shocked at coming upon accounts of mediæval miracles, and thinks at once that his credulity is being imposed upon; yet, he receives with the utmost calmness, and even satisfaction, a host of unauthenticated anecdotes about royal, or political, personages of the present or of past times. He would readily acknowledge that those are not strictly historical, but they assist him to gain a clearly defined idea of the persons to whom they relate; and, even when professedly fictitious, as in historical novels, he recognizes their usefulness, and never thinks of stigmatizing them as frauds or impostures. Even events of contemporary history, such as the miraculous incidents in the Life of the Curé of Ars, the apparition and the fountain of our Lady of Lourdes, the Stigmata of Louise Lateau, all of which are as capable of scientific criticism and verification, as any ordinary contemporaneous fact; yet, because they are of a supernatural character, they are even now thought by most Protestants unworthy of credit, and, had they appeared in any mediæval chronicle, they would certainly be regarded as utterly fabulous and incredible. The only difference between a Catholic and a Protestant in their estimation of such narratives, is that the Catholic has no antecedent conviction of the impossibility and falsity of the miracle related. If he makes any question at all about its historical certainty, he will be quite as exacting as a

Protestant in requiring strong evidence of
the truth of the story, but his mind will
generally be rather occupied with the
lesson conveyed by the legend, than with
the absolute credibility of the narrative
itself, and he will say, in the words of the
Italian proverb, *Se non è vero, è ben trovato.*
The legend brings home to the heart the
truths and aspirations of the Christian religion.   The narrative of the appearance of
saints in great glory stirs the heart to endure the cross through hope of the recompense to come.   The relation of the miracles which saints have wrought, causes the
heart to regard with wonder and reverence
the gifts of Christ in the Gospel dispensa-
tion.   And these legends assist us all in
realizing how closely the most ordinary acts
of life are bound up with our eternal in-
terests, and how slight is the veil that
hides from our view the great and all-
important, but too often forgotten realities
of the world to come.

LIFE OF ST. WILLIAM,

BISHOP OF BOURGES.

THE holy Bishop William of Bourges was born of noble parents, and from early childhood was given to his uncle, called Peter the Hermit, to be educated. He was made whilst a boy Canon of the Church of Paris, his uncle Peter being an Archdeacon. When he came to man's estate, quitting the world, he fled to the desert of Grandimont. But as some disturbance arose in that Order, he passed over to the Cistercian Monastery of Pontigni, where after his profession he was soon chosen Prior. He was then successively made Abbot of the Monasteries of John's Fountain and Charles' Place.

Now when the Archbishop Henry, of happy memory, had departed out of this light, the clergy of his Church met to consider of a successor. Not being able to agree, they referred the matter to the Archbishop of Paris, who had been elected to that dignity from their own body, and was a venerable and prudent man. They were however all agreed on this, that some Abbot of the Cistercian Order should be chosen, and the Blessed William was named by many. The Archbishop, in so momentous a matter, would decide nothing hastily. He placed under the cloth of the altar the names of all the Abbots designated, each name written on a sealed schedule. After he had offered the Adorable Sacrifice, and prostrated himself in prayer at the foot of the altar, he ascended to the altar, being wholly ignorant of the name each schedule contained, and from beneath the cloth he took one schedule. He opened it in the presence of two witnesses and found the name of William.

Meantime the clergy came to hear his decision. On entering into his presence many of them cried out, "It is the Abbot William." The Archbishop in gladness and admiration could not restrain his tears, as he exclaimed, "This is the Lord's doing." Thus was William chosen Archbishop and Primate of all Aquitaine. He alone was unwilling; but the Legate of the Apostolic See then in France commanded him to accept the burden, as laid upon him by the Will of God.

Thus forced to compliance, he, not without many tears, bade farewell to his Brethren, and went to Bourges. Here he was met by a great concourse of the people, and then solemnly consecrated by the Bishops.

In his new dignity he declined in nothing from the rigour of his life, that he might be able to say with the Apostle, " I chastise my body, and bring it into subjection, lest perhaps, when I have preached to others, I myself should become a castaway." In the midst of riches he was poor, and at splendid banquets knew what it was to be hungry. His clothing was for the covering of his body, not for pomp. Amidst those who went in soft clothing he wore his Monastic habit, glad to appear as a Monk rather than as a Bishop. He never wore less in summer nor more in winter. Though flesh-meat was on his table for the use of his guests, he never tasted of it himself.

Knowing that it was impossible to set others on fire, unless he were himself a burning coal, he not only refused unlawful things, but abstained gladly from things lawful. He bewailed the sins of others as if he had himself committed them, and was delighted with the prosperity of others, as though it was his own good fortune. With tears of compunction he washed away the slightest stains he was able to find in his inward man, that by his unblamable conversation and the word of his doctrine, he might cast out the beam of vice from the eyes of others. For he feared lest it might be justly said to him, " Physician, heal thyself." And even though not conscious to himself of anything, he still esteemed himself an unprofitable servant, ever suspicious and fearful, saying with the prophet, " Who understandeth

his transgressions ?   From my secret sins cleanse
Thou me, O Lord."

He shewed himself humble in proportion as by
his Episcopal office he was exalted in dignity,
according to the sentence of the Apostle, "Not
lording it over the clergy, but being made a pattern to the flock." He used especial diligence that
he might neither stain a virtuous life by perverse
doctrine, nor sound doctrine by a corrupt life.

Sometimes he appeared rather slack and indul-
gent towards offenders, but it was that by his
patience he might provoke them to repentance.
If however he found them obstinate, then flaming
with zeal he used the sword of chastisement, and
neither the threats of princes nor the blandish-
ments of friends could soften him. He suffered
not himself, like Heli, to be overcome by a false
pitifulness, but though he easily pardoned those
who mourned their offences, yet where it was
necessary he spared not the rod of discipline.
Thus he poured in oil and wine; wine to cleanse
the filth of the wound by its sharpness, and oil to
temper and soothe the pain.

He gave also great alms to the poor and needy,
knowing that the Lord loveth a cheerful giver,
compelling strangers and pilgrims to enter under
his roof. He visited also the sick and the prison-
ers, and those that were in the tertian or quartan
fevers. Many of these, hoping to receive a cure,
begged him to lay his hand upon them. This
he unwillingly consented to, lest he might be

esteemed a Saint. However, he would not entirely refuse, and some were immediately cured, others after a short while.

When making the circuit of his diocese a boy was brought to him, who for three months had been afflicted with a perpetual trembling of the head. He laid his hands on him, and in three days he was quite cured.

The old Enemy of the human race did not leave the holy Bishop unmolested, but strove especially to lift him up to pride, on account of the innocency of his life. The holy man, however, fled for refuge to the stronghold of the Lord, and routed the Enemy by the examples and sentences of the Divine Scriptures.

It was at that time the custom to inflict fines on those who were excommunicated, and some of the Bishops, even of great name, took this money for their private purse. The Enemy suggested to him that at least he might exact these fines for the benefit of the poor. But in this matter the holy man used great discretion and moderation, so that he might neither offend God nor give occasion of scandal to his neighbour. He neither condemned nor approved the custom of the country, but having enjoined a suitable satisfaction on the excommunicated persons, and taken security for the money, he absolved them and received them into the Church. As for the money, he never took it of them, though to strike them with a wholesome fear, he would threaten to do it, for he counted all the wealth of this world but as dung, having his treasure in heaven.

When he was advised to collect an army, and thus put down by arms the obstinate and incorrigible, so that the Church might in peace and tranquillity freely give herself to the divine offices, the examples of the Fathers and the custom of the country being urged to induce his consent, the holy man promised he would do something, lest he should seem rashly to condemn the practice of his forefathers. But he abhorred the shedding of blood. He liked not to lay waste the country, or to be surrounded with military weapons. He undertook to overcome the obdurate, not with material fire and sword, but with the sword of the Spirit, which is the word of God, and with threats of the fire of hell, with its burning pitch and sulphur. Nor was he disappointed of his hope, for, to the astonishment of many, these wolves suddenly became lambs, and those who before held him quite in contempt, now ran to his bidding as to that of their Pastor, calling him the holy Archbishop. And if any yet refused to obey him, they were looked at as no better than heathens.

At the beginning of his Pontificate he had to endure the anger of the King, whom wicked men inflamed against him, for defending the cause of the Church in temporal matters. The King's minions threatened to lay hands on his goods, and confiscate them to the King's use, unless he would reconcile himself to his offended Majesty. But this column neither could be shaken by terrors nor enfeebled by flatteries.

Between S. William and the Bishops of Tours and Paris there was a close and familiar friendship. They often visited each other, and communicated with each other concerning the care of the Churches and the salvation of souls. When, therefore, tidings were brought to him of the death of these his intimate and valued associates, he was greatly saddened. He survived them but a few months. But though by divine revelation he foreknew the day of his departure, it seemed long in coming, for he had a desire to be dissolved and to be with Christ. Whilst yet in the flesh, although through fasting his skin seemed to cleave to his bones, yet he ceased not to make his worn out body render its service to the spirit.

Christmas was now past, and on the Vigil of the Epiphany he desired, according to his old custom, to preach to the people. It was in the church of S. Stephen the First Martyr, and a great multitude of people had been gathered together. He took for his text, "Now is the hour to rise from sleep." As a last farewell he bade them to watch and pray, lest they should enter into temptation, and lest death, coming suddenly upon them, should find them unprepared. The winter cold was severe, and the place from whence he preached exposed to the

2

winds on every side ; his head also was uncovered.
On returning home a fever took him, which increased day by day. On the ninth of January he
received the Sacrament of Extreme Unction, and
begged then that he might have brought to him
the holy Eucharist, to be the Viaticum for his
journey. Although so enfeebled, yet when he
had notice that thus the Lord of Glory was coming to him, he quickly leapèd from the bed on
which he lay, and, by fervour of spirit gaining
strength, he went to meet Him, to the astonishment of those that were present. Then, throwing himself on his knees, his cheeks all flooded
with tears, he humbly adored his Saviour; and
that he might shew the more his love and worship, he rose several times from his knees, and
again bent them in adoring homage, commending
his last agony to the Lord, and begging of Him
that if still there were anything in him which
requ red purging, He would Himself be pleased
to purify it away, that the Enemy might find
nothing in him.

For two days before his death he was scarce
able to speak, and could with difficulty be understood by those who assisted him, except with the
aid of signs. Sometimes he prayed for a long
time prostrate. But when the Body of the Lord
was brought for his refection, he stretched forth
his arms in the form of a cross, his eyes raised up
to heaven, and his face bedewed with tears ; after
which, assisted by those who were with him, he

returned to his bed. He then signed to them
that after his death he wished his body to be
buried at Charles's Place, over which Monastery
he had long presided, and some of the Brothers
were present, who it is supposed had begged this
favour of him.

The others however remonstrated with him,
saying, "Far be it from us, holy Father, that we
should allow thy body to be taken away from thy
Church. We cannot consent to lose the presence
of that body which will always keep fresh in our
hearts the memory of so good a pastor. We beg
of thee therefore to remain yet with us, and by
thy merits and prayers to protect thy people when
dead, as thou hast watched over them when
living." He would not however give way to their
desires, but besought of them this liberty allowed
to all, to choose the place of his burial, which
they having unwillingly conceded, he kissed them
all, commending himself to their prayers, as they
likewise to his. The most of those present then
retired after receiving his blessing, for they feared
to be burdensome to him. His time was spent in
continual prayer, and his lips kept moving, as
though he were reciting psalms. On the night
before his death, he had brought forth the episcopal robes, in which he was consecrated, making
signs that he wished to be buried in them. The
holy old man was accustomed to rise each night
to recite the Vigils of the Divine Office, but fearing on this night that he might not live till the

fixed time for doing so, he wished to anticipate the hour. Giving therefore a signal to the Brethren, he signed himself with the sign of the cross, and pronounced the two words " *Domine labia,*" but he could go no farther. A priest who was his dear friend continued the words for him, and the Brethren recited the Office alternately with him, the Bishop joining in mind. This completed he desired to be laid on the ground, clad as he always was in a hair-shirt, though few knew it, and ashes strewed under him, in the form of a cross. He had but a little while lain thus, when, blessing the brethren for the last time, he gave up his spirit into the hands of his Creator.

The whole city was moved at the tidings of his death, and all of every age and sex thronged to the church of S. Stephen the First Martyr, to which the lifeless body was carried, with candles and torches, accompanied with the singing of hymns and canticles. Some who had despised his voice when living, now threw themselves prostrate before his corpse, not being ashamed openly to declare their penitence.

The next day there came a whole multitude out of the country places, as if to a festival day, leaving their houses unguarded, the doors open, and sometimes children in the cradle, so thoughtless was their eagerness to approach to the body of the holy Bishop. To their great joy, however, on their return no one had suffered any injury. On the funeral day no servile work was done, but all

with one accord came for a last look at the holy
body; to see the angelic face, and kiss his hands
and feet. To kiss them once was not enough, but
they would return again and again to do the
same.

On that day in the evening, when the whole
clergy and people were celebrating the funeral
service, there appeared over the Church of S.
Stephen a globe of light, having the appearance
of a glistening star. Not only did those who
were in the city behold it, but those also who
were approaching from without. It hung there
as it were suspended in the air for the space of
half an hour.

Meantime the bier was being prepared to carry
off the body to Charles' Place, the people as yet
knowing nothing of it. But when the thing
became known, it was universally determined by
the people that they would not suffer this to be
done. Accordingly an armed band kept watch
over every entrance to the Church, and a great
company remained in the Church the whole night.
The following morning was a Sunday. A deep
grave had been dug near to the Altar of S.
Stephen, and everything had been hastily prepared for the burial, it being intended that it
should take place before Mass. This however
could not be effected. So after Mass was over,
the Brothers from Charles's Place stood apart,
not knowing what to do, or what would come of
it. They dared not go near the body nor demand

liberty to remove it, for it had been decreed that
if any one should dare to lay hand on it, he
should pay with his life for the attempt.

Some of the most ancient of the priests of the
Church gave notice to the Brethren that there was
perfect liberty, as far as their consent was con-
cerned, that they should take away the holy body.
This they did the more freely, being certain that
the people would not suffer it. The Brothers at
last, seeing they could gain nothing, though sadly
disappointed of their hope, yielded to the people,
admiring their great devotion, and at least glad
that the body of the most Blessed man should
receive such an honourable burial.

On the very day of the funeral a miracle was
wrought which sufficiently bore testimony to the
sanctity of the holy Bishop. A boy not quite
ten years of age, whose whole body had been
bent double for three whole years, who could
neither walk, nor even lift his hand to his mouth,
hearing that the Bishop was dead, begged
earnestly of his mother to be carried to the
Church, that he might kiss the holy body. His
mother took him up in her arms, and entering the
Church, they both of them kissed his hands and
feet. The mother heard at that moment as it
were a crackling of his bones. When she was
going away with her burden, the boy cried: "Let
me walk, mother. I am cured by the merits of
the holy Bishop." The mother put him down on
his feet, and without any assistance he walked

home, to the admiration of all. The neighbours were all astonished, knowing the length of the boy's affliction. The mother, fearful of the great crowd at the Church, determined to delay returning thanks to the Saint, till the people were mostly gone. But as she waited the tidings of new miracles reached her ears, and unable to contain her gratitude, she took the boy by the hand, and both went off to the Church to join the rest.

After this, many others with various maladies and diseases came to be healed, and it would be too long to relate all. Suffice it to say, that the blind received their sight, the lame walked, the dropsical were healed, those possessed with devils were delivered. Sometimes these wonders occurred at the tomb of the Saint, sometimes by the simple invocation of a heart full of faith. Honorius III. after the requisite scrutiny, enrolled the Blessed man in the catalogue of canonised Saints.

LIFE OF BLESSED HENRY,

CARDINAL-BISHOP OF ALBE.

THE Blessed Henry was born of noble parents, in the province of Burgundy, in France. He gave himself, when quite young, to the Religious life, retiring to Clairvaulx in the year 1155, when Robert of Dunes guided the house. In the time of the next Abbot he was, four years after his profession, made Abbot of Haute Combe, for he had the wisdom of age though a youth in years, and his Monastery was blessed by God under his guidance, increasing in good discipline and in possessions.

Saint Gerard having been stabbed to death by a wicked Monk, whom he would have reformed, Henry was chosen in his place as Abbot of Citeaux. In this situation he strove to fulfil all justice, living as one of the Brethren, and sharing in their common labours. In this he was even excessive, for one day, during the time of the harvest, he was making hay in a farm across the river Aube, when tidings came in great haste that a Brother being ill asked for Extreme Unction. Henry, knowing that his presence encouraged the Brothers in their work, was unwilling to leave them, and sent another Priest of his Monks to give the last Sacraments to the sick Brother, who died shortly after.

Some days after the Brother had passed away to a better life, when the Blessed Henry was gone to his bed for rest, a certain Monk, who had died no long time before this other Brother, appeared to him in a visible form and said: "Know, Reverend Father, that the Brother who is lately dead, was, at the instant of his departure out of the flesh, presented by the Angels before the judgment seat of our Lord Jesus Christ, before Whom all his life had to be judged with much strictness. Now, when the Sovereign Judge was examining what had passed at the end of his life, question was made if all had been religiously observed in his regard, which is wont to be done for the dying. Answer was made that nothing had been wanting, except that the Abbot, being too much applied to labour, had not given himself Extreme Unction, but had had it administered by another. The Lord then bade me go and tell you from Him, that to do penance for this negligence you should say the Seven Penitential Psalms every day till your death." Having finished these words, the Monk disappeared. The Blessed Henry was not a little astonished. He saw from this that the Lord God has care of all, little as well as great. He fulfilled his penance punctually, even after he was Cardinal Bishop, never omitting it, and he used to say to his friends that he would rather abstain from saying Mass at Christmas or Easter than miss reciting the Seven Penitential Psalms.

There was another Brother at Clairvaulx, who had come from another Monastery in penance for a great crime he had committed, which he never would tell in confession. But when death came upon him he cried out in the middle of the night for a Confessor. The Blessed Henry immediately came. The poor Brother then confessed his sin, saying that he had just been led down into hell in spirit, where he saw the torments he would have to endure so soon as he was removed from this world. The Reverend Father told him that no one ought to despair so long as he is in this life, but have confidence in the infinite mercies of God. He then gave him a suitable penance, and comforting his heart a little, gave him absolution, and went back to the Dormitory.

He had scarcely been there an hour when the poor Brother again sent for him : and as soon as he came in, cried out that he had been a second time conducted in spirit to the place of punishment in the next world. He had been told that he had indeed escaped the pains of hell, but that he would have to pay the last farthing in purgatory in expiation of his crimes. Then he confessed to having received of a Brother a robe without permission, which he had never confessed as a sin against poverty. Having received absolution, he died in calm shortly after.

Now in the year of grace 1179, Pope Alexander

III. held at Rome the Œcumenical Council of
Latran, where three hundred Bishops were assembled, and a great number of Abbots, of whom
Henry was one. Before the Council was over
Henry was compelled to yield to the authority of
the Pope, who made him Cardinal-Bishop of
Albe. In this dignity he preserved the same
spirit he had before, using herbs and legumes for
his diet, and his greatest dainty was a few small
fish of an ordinary kind.

The Pope sent him to preach the cross in Germany. He took with him several Monks of his
Order. Now one day, as they were altogether, he
said : "Which of you will tell us something
edifying?" Then, taking a Convert Brother, he
set him in the midst, and said, "You shall tell
us something." The Brother, who was new to
the Cardinal, and did not know the strict mortifi-
cation of his life, thought to give him quietly a
hint of his duty, and spoke as follows.

"When we are dead and conducted to the
gates of Paradise, our Father Saint Benedict will
come to meet us, and when he sees us Monks in
our Monastic dress, he will welcome us with
great joy. But when he sees the Cardinal-
Bishop Henry in his fine clothing, he will say,
'Ha! who are you?' Then Henry will answer,
'I am a Monk of the Cistercian Order.' But
Saint Benedict will answer, 'Not at all. A Monk
does not wear horns on his head.' Then Henry,
saying what he can to justify himself, Saint

Benedict will address the gatekeepers of Paradise after this manner : ' Put this man on his back, and open his stomach ; if you find in it beans, peas, lentils, and other similar things, let him enter with the Monks into Paradise. If, on the contrary, you find in it large fish, and well-seasoned meats, such as men of the world eat, leave him outside.' " Then, turning to the Cardinal, he said, " What will poor Henry do then ?" The Cardinal gave him a smile of satisfaction, well content with the simplicity of his speech.

The Blessed Henry, having given the cross to a multitude of persons in Germany, returned to Liege. Here six hundred Priests gave up their benefices into his hands, fearing they had obtained them by simony. He thence went to Flanders, though very ill in health, to reconcile the Count of Flanders, and the Church of Arras. As his sickness increased, he received the last Sacraments at the hands of the Bishop of Arras, himself a Cistercian Monk. As his last moments approached, he caused himself to be carried into the Church, where, before the Altar of S. Andrew, he breathed forth his spirit. His body was by his own order carried to Clairvaulx, where it was laid with all honour by the Bishop of Langres, between those of Saint Bernard and Saint Malachy. He died on the eleventh of January, A.D. 1189.

LIFE OF BLESSED WILLIAM,

ONCE ABBOT OF SAINT THEODORIC, AFTERWARDS
MONK OF CLAIRVAULX.

THE Abbot William in early youth embraced
the sacred state of Religion in the Cloister
of S. Theodoric, a Cluniac Monastery. So strict
was he that he would rather have parted with his
life than break the smallest of the constitutions
of his Fathers. His example was of profit to
many. Soon after his conversion he was made
Abbot of his house. It was at this time that the
glorious Father Bernard laid the foundations of
Clairvaulx in Campania. The fame of this Saint
reached the ears of Blessed William, who, being a
man of desires, longed much for the friendship of
so great a Father. He could not rest till he had
visited Clairvaulx, and enjoyed somewhat of the
company of the holy Father. At that time the
Abbot Bernard, compelled by the authority of his
Bishop, dwelt in a little house apart. "Here,"
says William, "I found him, exulting as it were
in the delights of Paradise. And when I entered
that royal chamber, and considered the habitation,
and him that dwelt in it, I was struck with as
great a reverence as if I had been approaching to
the altar of God. I was affected with such sweet-

ness towards that man, and with such a desire of dwelling in that poverty and simplicity with him, that, had the choice been allowed me, there is nothing I should have preferred to remaining for the rest of my life to serve him. He also received me with joy, and when I asked him how he did, he said, 'Excellently well. Up to this time rational men obeyed me, now, by the just judgment of God, I am tied to obey a rational beast.' This he said of a vain country charlatan, who, knowing nothing, had boasted he could cure him; and this man he was bound to obey by commandment of his Bishop, and of the Abbots his Brethren. When I there ate with him, and thought how one so sick should be delivered over to such hands, and when, moreover, I saw the food which this physician offered him, food which even a healthy man would scarce have eaten if pressed hard by hunger, I felt quite faint, and could hardly restrain myself from breaking the rule of silence at mealtime, and reproaching this man as a sacrilegious manslayer. He however for whom I felt, took all things indifferently, approving all equally, as one who, his taste being almost dead, scarce discerned one thing from another. For indeed he is known to have drunk oil, when offered to him, instead of water."

Is it wonderful that the Blessed William desired to be enrolled in the company of Clairvaulx, beholding the sanctity of so great a Father? Nor was it in the Abbot alone that he observed it.

In that golden age the Monastery of Clairvaulx was, as it were, the Paradise of pleasure of the Church of God, bearing richest fruits of beauty and renown.

"At the first look," says Blessed William, "God is known in her dwellings by all who, descending the mountain, enter Clairvaulx. The simplicity and lowliness of the buildings speaks with mute voice of the simplicity and humility of Christ's poor, who dwell therein. In that valley, where no one is idle, all being occupied in the work appointed them, the silence of midnight is found at midday. The only noise heard is the sound of labour, or the voices of the Brethren singing the praise of God. Even strangers on a visit have such reverence for this silence that they would fear to utter a useless word, much more an idle and unseemly one. The very loneliness of the place itself, amidst the dark shadows of the neighbouring woods and mountains, makes the place where these Brethren lie hid like the cave, in which the holy Father Benedict was discovered by the shepherds. Though the valley is full of men, yet in the midst of this multitude they lead a solitary life, through the quietude of their souls, just as a disordered man is a tumultuous crowd to himself.

"Their food is as simple as their dwellings. Their bread, won with hardest toil by the Brethren from a barren soil, is so black that one would suppose it were mingled with earth rather

than with bran. What else they eat has scarce
any savour, but what hunger and the love of God
can give it. The zeal of their spiritual Father
has made delightful many things, which formerly
seemed impossible to men made of flesh and
blood. Nay, they feel a temptation to murmur
because their life is so delightful. They suspect
that they are being defrauded of the crown promised to them that endure hardness. For the
grace of God, like the meal mingled in the pot by
the prophet Eliseus, taking away its natural
bitterness, renders everything delightful to their
taste."

Seeing then so many graces and virtues in
those of Clairvaulx, stirring him up to the desire
of a more perfect life, the Blessed William earnestly longed to give himself up to the guidance
of the most holy Abbot Bernard. Bernard himself was much afflicted when William left him to
return to his own Abbey. Above all those who
were intimate with him he loved William the
best, admiring the holy purity of his soul.
William was a man possessed by a great desire to
understand the hidden things of the Scriptures.
For this reason his companionship was sweet
and very grateful to the holy Father Bernard.
So great a joy was his presence to him, and so
much did he hold to him, that on a time when
the most holy Father had fallen into a perilous
sickness, knowing that William also was sick in
bed, he sent for him, asking him to come, telling

him also that if he would come to Clairvaulx he
would recover from sickness; but that, even if
God ordained it otherwise, at least he would be
buried among friends. Gerard, Bernard's own
brother, carried the message, and so pleased was
William with the two promises contained in it,
that, making no account of his sickness, or of the
difficulties of the journey, he at once, with Gerard
as companion, set out on his road to Clairvaulx.
He knew that by doing so he exposed his life to
danger; it was enough however that the holy
Father Bernard had asked him. Bernard, on his
arrival, rose as well as he could to greet him with
the kiss of peace. William soon recovered his
health at Clairvaulx, and his presence was the
greatest consolation to the holy Father Bernard in
a long sickness. For by the sweetness of his
company he forgot the pains with which he was
afflicted. Together they fulfilled the task of the
Divine Office; together they took their meals,
and when they had given thanks to God, the
greater part of the day was passed in treating of
the Sacred Scriptures, the glorious Bernard, to
William's delight, expounding the moral and
mystical sense. It happened one night, that
having opened the Canticle of Canticles, William
asked for an exposition of it, when the holy
Father spoke in so heavenly a manner that,
although he listened with all attention, the words
were too high for his comprehension. He begged
therefore the holy man to abate somewhat the

3

loftiness of his flight. William, receiving thus all the words from his mouth, caused them afterwards to be written down by others. It was through these explications that he composed those divine discourses on the Canticles which he left behind him.

In this manner the days passed till Septuagesima. The Blessed William wished at this time to return to his own Abbey; Bernard, however, would not hear of his leaving till Quinquagesima was passed. Now as William found that he could rise and go about without assistance, he wished from the time of Septuagesima to give up all use of flesh meat. "The holy Abbot Bernard, however," he says, "forbad me. Upon this point, however, I would neither listen to his counsel, nor hear his entreaties, nor obey his commands. On Saturday evening we parted from each other, I to my couch, he to go to Compline in silence. But all that night I lay tormented with the vehement ferocity of my disease, which, rising as it were from the dead, poured out all its malignity upon me. In the early morning I sent for the man of God, for I was so spent that I despaired of life. He came, not with his usual compassion, but with the face of a reprover, asking me, however, with a smile, 'What will you eat to-day?' I from his silence interpreted that my disobedience of the day before was the cause of my affliction, so I answered, 'I will eat what you bid me.' 'Well,' he answered, 'be at peace, you will not die yet.'

And so he departed. And then all at once my pains left me; but so tired was I that I could scarce rise from bed all the day. Oh what pains were those. I never remember to have suffered the like at any time. The next day, however, I felt quite in health, and after a few more days' delay, I departed, with the blessing of my good host, to my own Abbey."

The taste for Cistercian quiet, which he had experienced at Clairvaulx, was such that with importunate prayers he desired to be admitted to the Cistercian habit, laying aside his dignity of Abbot. The Father Bernard, however, delayed making any answer to his request; but later on he told him that he should indeed end his days in the Cistercian profession; for the present it was more advisable that he should rule well his own flock, and study their profit, not shrinking from his burden. The Blessed William was consoled by this promise, and sought meantime to bring into his own Cloister the mortified spirit he had seen at Clairvaulx. This bond of love which mutually cemented the hearts of himself and of the most holy Father Bernard, caused them frequently to interchange letters of friendship with each other, to give some vent at least to their tenderness, since the care of the souls entrusted to their charge prevented their continual companionship.

The letters of Blessed William were the most frequent, because that the holy Abbot of Clairvaulx, occupied with the affairs of the Church, had not sufficient leisure to satisfy the demands of private friendship. William therefore says that less love is returned to him than what he himself gives so plenteously. Bernard, in a beautiful Epistle, thus answers his complaint.

"If it be true that 'no man knoweth the things of a man, except the spirit of a man that is in him;' if man seeth only in the face, for that God alone beholdeth the heart, I wonder, nor can I enough wonder, how or by what method you have been able to weigh the love we have one to the other, or to pronounce not only concerning your own heart, but even to give judgment concerning that of another. Since the mind of man sometimes mistakes good for evil, and evil for good, takes truth for falsehood and falsehood for truth, certain things for doubtful, and doubtful for certain, that which thou sayest may be true : that my love of you is less than your love of me. It may be true, but of this I am certain, that you can have no certainty of it. How then affirm for certain that of which it is certain you cannot be certain? An astonishing thing! Paul did not trust himself to his own judgment: 'Neither do I judge myself,' he says. Peter bewails his own presumption, by which he had been deceived concerning himself, saying, 'If I must die with Thee I will not deny Thee.' The disciples, even in the betrayal of the Lord, did not trust in their own consciences, but answered, 'Lord, is it I?' David

confesses his ignorance concerning himself, when
he prays, saying, 'Remember not my ignor-
ances.' You, however, with strange confidence,
must know not only your own heart, but mine
too, complaining thus openly, 'Loving more I am
less loved.' These are your words. And would
they were not, for I know not whether they be
true. If you know the source of your knowledge,
where is your proof that you love me more than I
you? Is it this which you subjoin, that those
who come to you from me bring you no token of
love from me? What token of love do you
require? Are you uneasy because I have but
once written back to several of your letters?
How should I think to give you pleasure with my
unskilful scribblings? For I know who it was
that said, 'My little children, let us not love in
word nor in tongue, but in deed and in truth.'
When was any deed of love necessary to you and
I was found wanting? O Thou Who searchest
the hearts and reins, Who, as the one Sun of
Justice with diverse rays of grace, enlightenest
the hearts of Thy servants, Thou knowest that
through Thy gift and from his own merit I love
him, my own heart being conscious of it. How
much I love him Thou knowest, but I know not.
Thou, Who hast given this love, knowest how
much Thou hast given him to love me, and me to
love him, and how shall either of us dare to say,
'being less loved I love more,' unless it be that
in Thy light he sees his own light, that is, he in

the light of Thy truth perceives how much he loves. I am content in Thy light to see my own darkness, until Thou shalt visit me, sitting in darkness and the shadow of death, and by Thee the thoughts of the hearts shall be revealed, and the hidden things of darkness made manifest."

It may be well seen from the above, what a love it was which united these two servants of Christ in the bond of charity.

Blessed William so lost hold of earthly things in his contemplation of the things above, that sometimes all sense of them departed from him. His eyes fixed on the ground, his whole soul was caught up with vehemence into heaven.

His charity to the poor was such, that oftentimes he gave away the food necessary for the sustenance of the Brethren. There came a man to him, asking for wine, which he wanted as medicine. There was scarce left what might serve for the Altar. Nevertheless he ordered it to be given. The Steward, fearing there would not be wine for the Mass, excused himself to the poor man, telling him that none could be spared, lest wine should be wanting for the holy Mass. The Abbot, however, having met the poor man, asked him if he had received the wine. He answered that it had been refused him by the Steward. The holy man was displeased at this disobedience. He called for the Steward, and bidding him give to the poor man what wine was in the vessel, ordered also that which was in the cask to be poured out of the window, saying that God would not permit wine kept by disobedience to be dedicated to the Sacrifice of the Eucharist. God was not wanting in shewing His acceptance of the zeal of His servant. A rich cleric who lived hard by the Monastery at that moment entered the gate, having a horse loaded with wine and other provisions. The Abbot, seeing this, called for the Steward, and publicly chid him for his disobedience, telling him always to trust in God, and he would surely reap his reward.

The Blessed William was present at the glorious passage of the most holy Father Bernard from his earthly tabernacle. His sorrow for this separation was somewhat softened by the frequent visits he received from the departed Saint. Soon after he laid aside his office of Abbot, and received at Clairvaulx the Cistercian habit, beginning at the same time a life of such austerity that his past life seemed to him nothing but imperfections. He also began to write, in his beautiful style, the Life of S. Bernard, being an eye-witness of many of his graces and miracles. God, however, called him to Himself, A.D. 1160, and as some say, on the twelfth of January. His passage was full of signs of glory, certain miracles were wrought before his burial, and his name was enrolled in the Catalogue of Cistercian Saints.

LIFE OF

BLESSED GEOFFREY OF PERONNE,

PRIOR OF CLAIRVAULX.

GEOFFREY of Peronne came of an illustrious Flemish family. He was a man of great wealth, and whilst yet young was made Bursar of the Church of S. Quentin. When the holy Father Bernard visited Flanders in A.D. 1131, Geoffrey, with others, to the number of twenty-nine, amongst whom were some men of great talents, were so touched by the marvels they saw and heard that without delay they resolved to quit the world, and place their souls under his guidance. They wrote a letter to the Blessed Father, telling him their sentiments. He on his part wrote to them, praising their resolution, and telling them to have confidence. Whilst some little delay kept them settling their affairs, the arch-enemy of souls filled their minds with the greatest repugnance for the state of Religion, and it required a second letter from him to dissipate the wiles of the Wicked One. The most holy Bernard wrote a special letter to the parents of Geoffrey, who were striving all they could to prevent their son from embracing the Monastic state.

Now when Geoffrey was on his road to Clairvaulx, in company with the most holy Abbot and some of his Monks, one of them, casting his eyes on him, saw by the sadness of his countenance the tempest of his mind. "Why," said this Brother to him, "is your countenance fallen, and covered with a dark cloud?" "Ah!" said Geoffrey, "I shall never know what joy is any more." The Brother hearing this, entered into a Church, which was by the side of the road, on which they were travelling, and began to pray, whilst the rest waited outside. Geoffrey, weary with sadness, fell asleep, and the Brother, having prayed awhile, came and woke him. But if he entered the Church in sadness, he departed from it with a heart bounding with joy of the Holy Ghost, so completely had he been changed by the Right Hand of the Most High.

There came back to Clairvaulx with the holy Abbot almost a hundred gentlemen, from Flanders and elsewhere, to whom with Geoffrey and his company he gave the Monastic habit, exhorting them to persevere in the grace of God, which they had so abundantly received.

The Blessed Geoffrey, not content with his own salvation, was earnest in his desires for that of his father. He therefore besought the Blessed Abbot to pray for his conversion. "Fear not," said the man of God to him, "I shall see him a Monk of this house, and shall bury him with my own hands." Both these things came to pass, for he became a monk at Clairvaulx, and falling ill of his last sickness when the most holy Abbot was away from the Monastery, he continued so for five months, often seeming on the point of departure, till the man of God having returned, he quietly passed away in peace, and received the last rites at his hands, according as had been promised.

The Blessed Geoffrey, having pronounced his vows A.D. 1132, was eight years after made Prior of Clairvaulx. He held this office till he passed away in the year of redemption, 1146.

A year before his happy passage he was elected, says Peter de Blois, Bishop of Tournay, but he would by no means consent to the election. The most Blessed Father Bernard, and even the Pope Eugenius, in vain commanded him to accept, he remained firm in his resistance, and they were forced to yield and to be silent. He lived only a few months longer. His death was a source of the greatest affliction to his Brethren, for they loved him dearly, and he, on his part, returned their love with an extraordinary affection.

In proportion as they loved him they feared for his disobedience, and thought what judgment he might meet with from the hands of the Most High God. They were not long left in doubt. The Blessed man appeared to one of them a few days after his death, and the glory of God shone round about him. Being asked whether he had received any punishment for his disobedience, he replied, that not only had he not been punished, but that God had made known to him that had he accepted the Bishopric he would certainly have lost his soul.

LIFE OF HUGH, BISHOP OF AUXERRE.

HUGH de Mâçon was a native of Burgundy, joining nobility of blood with nobleness of soul, and a high courage, which made him much esteemed in that elevated rank which he held in the world.

God drew him from the world by means of the close friendship he had contracted with the great and holy Father Bernard. It is true he resisted the call given to him and strove to draw himself back, but He who had chosen him out of the world for His own glory would not suffer him to remain entangled in its corruptions.

He was at first so far from having any desire to follow the example of his friend, that, on the contrary, he wept for him as for one dead. The Lord of all things, however, holding in His Hand the wills of men, and giving them what movement He pleases, knew well how to change his thoughts. As it is natural for friends to desire to converse with one another, the heart of Hugh could not resist its longing to seek the society of Bernard. The two friends wept at their first meeting, but their tears came from very different sources. They then entered into conversation, each speaking of his own aims, speaking out one

to the other, heart to heart. They ended by
clasping each the hand of the other in mutual
agreement to join in a new life.

These first sentiments of conversion, however,
did not last long. The false friends of Hugh
soon blew away all his good resolutions. And
when Bernard wished again to rescue his companion from his peril these false friends gave him
no liberty of conversing with him alone. Bernard, however, prayed to God, and God heard
him. When a great party were out in the country, among whom were Bernard and Hugh,
although the sky had appeared so serene that
there appeared no danger of rain, on a sudden the
air became filled with a storm of clouds. All
took to flight to a neighbouring village, except
Bernard and Hugh. As Hugh was going with
the rest, Bernard laid hold of him by the hand,
saying, " You must stop and dry up this rain
with me." And they two remained alone. The
storm passed away almost immediately without
breaking, and there in that place they renewed
their first purpose, giving to each other inviolable
promises.

Hugh followed the Blessed Bernard to Citeaux.
He was soon afterwards made Abbot of Pontigni.
In A.D. 1136, he was made Bishop of Auxerre.
He did much public service in the difficulties of
the Church, and was a strong opposer of the
errors of Gilbert of Porree. He passed to his

reward at Pontigni, October 10, A.D. 1151, and was buried near the High Altar of the Church. In A.D. 1560 his body was found uncorrupted. The Calvinists, taking it for that of S. Edmund, Archbishop of Canterbury, impiously burnt it to ashes.

LIFE OF

BLESSED GEOFFREY OF AMAIE,

MONK OF CLAIRVAULX.

GEOFFREY of Amaie was one of those who, leaving the world, retired with the most holy Bernard to the Cloister of Citeaux. He was sent with him to Clairvaulx at the foundation of that Abbey. The most holy Father held him in great esteem, and employed him in the foundation of numerous Monasteries, knowing his great virtue, wisdom, and prudence, and his zeal for the observance of the Rule. Geoffrey having a great desire to die at Clairvaulx, in the arms of his beloved Father, would never consent to be Abbot of any of the Monasteries he founded, but when he saw that things were in a good state at the new Monasteries, and that his presence was no longer required, he quickly returned to Clairvaulx.

It was he who taught the Monastic observance of Citeaux to the Abbey of Fountains in England. When he was sent on this expedition, although he received the order with submission, yet he thought it not against obedience to represent to his beloved Father the pain he experienced at the thought, that being now advanced in years, it

might chance that he should die out of Clairvaulx, where he desired to lay his body to rest.
The most Blessed Father, seeing his distress,
took pity on him, and said to him : "Fear not:
you shall be buried by me in this Monastery."
Assured by this promise, Geoffrey went with a
good heart, and having fulfilled his task, made
haste back to Clairvaulx, that he might have the
happiness‾of breathing his last in the arms of his
beloved Father. "I go," he said, "to die at
Clairvaulx." And so indeed it was ; for scarcely
had he returned when he found himself taken
with a most grievous sickness, which in a very
short while brought him to the gates of death.
The Blessed and most holy Father Bernard was
absent at the time of his return, having been
obliged to go on a journey to Trêves. It seemed
as if his promised word would not be accomplished. But not so. The sick man still lin-
gered on, as it were waiting for the fulfilment of
this word.

Whilst he thus hung between life and death,
and the Blessed Father Bernard had no thought
of returning, it pleased the Lord to reveal to him
the state in which his beloved Geoffrey lay. This
took place in the following manner. He had a
vision in his sleep, and he beheld his uncle
Gaultry and his brother Gerard, both of whom
had now been dead some years, passing by him as
if in great haste. When he wished to retain
them awhile, they excused themselves, saying that

they could not stay, as they were going to assist at the death of Geoffrey, their ancient comrade, who for the honour of God had been employed in founding such a number of Monasteries. He then seemed to see them present at the passing of Geoffrey from this earth, making ready to conduct his soul to heaven as soon as it should have gone forth from the body. When the holy Father complained to them of their cruelty in taking away Geoffrey from him, not content with having abandoned him themselves, they answered with a smile, that it was not for them to make any reply on these matters.

Waking up out of his sleep, he at once started on his journey, and on arriving at Clairvaulx he found the Blessed man just in the state he had seen him in his vision, and though he could not see Gaultry and Gerard, he did not doubt that they also were really present. It was enough for the holy old man. He embraced his beloved Father once more, and breathed forth his spirit in his sweet company. He passed to his rest on the twenty-first of January, A.D. 1150, having been a Monk forty years.

LIFE OF SAINT GUERRIN,

BISHOP OF SION.

THE Monastery of the Alps was founded by Humbert, Count of Savoy, in the diocese of Geneva. The Monks of this Abbey followed the Rule of S. Benedict. The Blessed Guerrin was Abbot at the time when the name of the most holy Father Bernard became famous in the earth by his life and miracles. The birthplace of the Abbot Guerrin was a little town of Lorraine, called Pont-a-Mousson. He came of high lineage, and it is said embraced the Monastic state first at Molême, and afterwards became Abbot of the Monastery of the Alps. He was a man full of the Spirit of God, and a person of no ordinary prudence. His zeal in the service of God was such that at an advanced age the weakness of his body in nowise lessened the vigour of his mind, nor hindered him in procuring the benefit of his Brethren. Nay, the force of his words and example was enhanced by the veneration due to his age.

The holiness of the father shed its rays on the children, and warmed them into the desire of perfection. Embracing all the observance of their Rule, they followed the advice of their Abbot, and giving up the separate cells to which they had been accustomed, they began to live the common life, using one common room as a sleeping place. They also gave up all other practices contrary to the purity of the Rule they had professed. In the year of our Lord 1136, they ended by subjecting their Abbey to that of Clairvaulx. The most holy Abbot Bernard sent to them several of his Monks, to form them to the Cistercian Observance, the Blessed Guerrin still remaining in the place of Abbot. He also sent to the Blessed Guerrin a letter full of unction and charity, which greatly consoled and edified \the holy Brethren.

Two years after this, the clergy of Sion, in Switzerland, elected the Blessed Guerrin to be their Bishop. Upon the refusal of the holy man to accept this charge, recourse was had to the Sovereign Pontiff, who commanded him to undertake it. Guerrin wrote to His Holiness a letter of excuse, but the Pope was persistent in his command, and therefore the holy man felt compelled to yield to the pressure.

The most Blessed Father Bernard wrote to the Brethren in their affliction after this sort: " Your holy Father, who is also our Father too, has been raised by the will of God to a higher degree. For us, my dear Brethren, let us do as says the Prophet. The sun was raised up, and the moon remained in its order. Your holy Father is truly a sun, through which your Monastery has become luminous with splendour on all sides. Now that he is raised up, it is for us to remain in our Order, us who have better loved to be despised in the house of our God than to dwell in the tents of the wicked.

"Now our Order is abjection, lowliness, voluntary poverty, obedience, peace and joy in the Holy Ghost. Our Order is to submit to a Superior, to live under an Abbot, under a rule, under exact discipline. Our Order is to keep a strict silence, to exercise ourselves in watching, fasting, prayer, and labours of the hands, but especially and above all, in the most perfect and excellent way of charity."

It is needless to say how carefully the Blessed Guerrin fulfilled that office, from the burden of which he shrank. He never, however, forgot his solitude of the Alps, and from time to time visited the place, in order to taste there the happiness of silence and retreat.

It was in one of these visits that God was pleased to hear his prayers, that he might be removed from this workshop of the body. Having remained several days at the Abbey, he became ill. His zeal, however, getting the better of his weakness, he started on his journey back to Sion. When, however, he was come to a mountain called Mont de Tey, he could get no further. God, willing that he should finish his earthly sojourning in his Monastery, by the wonderful working of His Right Hand, caused the feet of the mule on which the Bishop rode should bury themselves deep in a hard rock, as if it had been so much wax. At the same time the Abbey bells pealed out, rung by no mortal hand. This double prodigy left no doubt on the holy Bishop's mind that it was the will of God he should return to the Abbey. He did so, and falling sick, in a short while he cast off the burden of the flesh, passing to his rest on the sixteenth of January. His feast, however, is kept by the Swiss people on the twenty-eighth of August.

His body reposes at the bottom of the Quire in the Church of the Alps, in a sepulchre of marble, raised on four pillars. It is a place of pilgrimage from all the neighbouring provinces, an innumerable crowd coming every day to gain the benefit of his intercession. In A.D. 1689, the Calvinist Waldenses, passing by the Abbey of the Alps, pillaged it, profaning the altars, and treading under foot the holy relics of the Saints. They tried with hammers and other instruments to break down the tomb of the man of God. But the Most High sent upon them a sudden fear. The bell of the Church sounded seven strokes of itself, and these miserable men, mounting to the turret, and searching on all sides without being able to find any one, were seized with dread, and fled quickly out of the Church. This miracle was attested by many who were present.

Among other relics thrown into the fire was the

Mitre of the man of God, but though the fire was made exceeding hot, it was in no way hurt.

God honours His servant to this very day by a number of miracles wrought at his tomb. Many have been worked by a key, which, it is said, was presented to the holy Bishop by the Pope. It is in great veneration throughout Savoy, Burgundy, and Frieburg. It is reported that the touch of it frees men and beasts from all sorts of sicknesses.

It is not certain in what year the Blessed Guerrin died, but it is probably conjectured to have been, A.D. 1142.

LIFE OF THE BLESSED CHARLES,

ABBOT OF HEMMENRODE.

THE Blessed Charles was a native of Germany, a man of high rank and ancient family, being sprung from the Landgraves of Scyne and Fustenburg, distinguished families in Westphalia in the time of Charlemagne. By profession a soldier, he was so renowned in arms that Philip, Archbishop of Cologne, when in fear of his life from Frederic Barbarossa, chose him for his protector from the violence of that King.

As Charles was returning from a tournament at Worms with Gerard von Wascard, they came to a most pleasant meadow, full of various flowers of every hue, and watered with springs and rivers. They passed through this fair meadow, neither speaking to the other. When they had, however, gone through, each one asked the other what his thoughts had been. One said: "I thought of and considered diligently the wonderful and varied beauties of this pleasant place, and the issue of all this was that I saw how vain and of little moment all the flourish of the world is." The other answered: "I had just the same thoughts." Then they said to one another: " These thoughts, with which we have been favoured, must not be fruitless to us. Let us cross the seas and fight against the foes of Christ. But then we should meet there the same things we leave here; fine horses and armour, and the beauty of women would wound our hearts, and perhaps we might lose our chastity. What then? Suppose we pass to Hemmenrode, and there beg five years' delay to visit tournaments." They made then a conditional vow that both would become Monks in the same Cloister. When they returned to Cologne, the whole city, by the incitation of the devil, reproached them with the folly of their vow. They left Cologne for Liege, where Ulric Flasco tried to draw them to cross the seas. Not prevailing with them, he vowed to be a Monk with them. There Gerard had a portion of his hand cut off. He said he was pleased that it had happened to him rather than to Charles, who was a cleric, and whom he hoped one day to see a priest.

A short time being now past, in A.D. 1183, being thirty years old, Charles left his parents, and his worldly goods, and entered the holy warfare in the Cloister of Hemmenrode. By his example he drew with him Ulric Flasco, Gerard von Wascard, Walter von Birbach, and others, among whom was Herman, Canon of Bonne. This man was afterwards Abbot of Hemmenrode. When he entered the Convert brothers' choir at the singing of the *Te Deum*, to rouse them, one of them, named Henry, saw a snow-white dove descend on his head, and remain there till he left the choir. The dove then rested on the cross of their Altar. When the Abbot mounted to the pulpit to read the Gospel the dove flew to the same place, and returned to the cross at the " *Te decet laus,*" after which it was seen no more. The same Henry saw a dove of wonderful beauty hovering over Charles when he received the habit of Novice.

In the year 1188, in the month of April, a Community went forth from Hemmenrode, with the Abbot Herman, to Mount Stroorberch, at the petition of the Archbishop of Cologne, to found the Monastery of Heisterbach. The Blessed Charles went with him. Here Godescalch, Canon of Cologne, gave himself with Albert, Canon and Bursar of the same Church, to the Abbot Herman, telling no one beforehand of his purpose. It happened that his brother Everard was in Westphalia on a journey, and made a visit to a holy woman, a recluse, in a rock. She received him with great humility and alacrity, and after some edifying words she said, " Tell your brother Godescalch that his light is kindled before the Lord, and shines exceedingly." His brother, hearing this, was amazed, knowing that Godescalch had hitherto been much given to a worldly life. He said therefore to the recluse : " See, sister, what you would say. Such a one as you speak of is not like my brother, who is given only to worldly luxury and amusements." He then by many prayers drew from her all she meant.

" Thus and thus," said she, " God has wrought, but the light of one is not yet kindled." Everard was struck with sorrow, being a man given to the world, and on his return to Cologne he found that Godescalch had indeed joined the Monks of Heisterbach. Albert was not yet gone. He went after some years, but died whilst a Novice.

The Blessed Charles, by the sweetness of his example, won many from a worldly conversation, and caused them to embrace Religious poverty, whence a certain knight, speaking to Herman the Abbot, wondered how it was that men of rank, nurtured in delicacies, could be brought to live on a diet of beans, peas, lentils, and such like food. The Abbot replied : " I mix three grains of pepper in this food, which gives it a relish which it has not in itself. The first grain is labour of the hands, the second is long watches, the third the hopelessness of obtaining anything better."

The Abbot of Villers William having passed to a better life in A.D. 1197, Charles was elected in his room. He at first refused to accept the office, but was compelled by a command of the General Chapter. He found the buildings of the Abbey exceedingly miserable, like the cabins of shepherds. In a short while, however, he built two Dormitories of stone, and enlarged the Granges. He knew so well how to fit himself to all dispositions and ranks, that he converted many, both noble and ignoble, among whom was the Blessed Conrad, afterwards a Cardinal Bishop.

The sister of the Blessed Charles became a Nun of the Cistercian Order. Being of an age to marry, and being sought by several suitors, she one day beheld the most blessed Virgin Mary standing by her, who, placing a wreath of most beautiful flowers on her head, presently disappeared. The pious maid was amazed at what had happened, and taking counsel on the matter from a Cistercian Abbot, she fled from her home to the convent of Dunewarch, where she received the Regular habit, and lived most holily to the end of her life.

After great labours, the Blessed Charles with many prayers obtained permission from the Abbot of Clairvaulx to retire from his office. Very unwilling was the Abbot to grant this permission, yet he felt unable to refuse him. "This man," he said, "is honoured by the sovereign princes of the earth. He is cherished and beloved in his own Monastery. He has enlarged his house in buildings and possessions, and the vigour of Religion has not relaxed under his rule. Great and honoured persons have become Monks in his Abbey. They cannot, however, keep him any longer in his office now that he has conquered me."

The Blessed Charles retired to Hemmenrode.

The day of his departure to the heavenly country is marked in the Cistercian Menology on the 29th of January.

LIFE OF BLESSED ALAN,

MONK OF CITEAUX.

THE Blessed Alan was a native of Lisle, in Flanders, and before his conversion, Doctor of the University of Paris, where he had taught theology. He was called the universal Doctor, because there was nothing to which his knowledge did not extend. He had a perfect knowledge of the Hebrew, Greek, and Latin languages. He was well instructed in Canon and Civil law. He knew what are called the seven liberal arts. He excelled in poesy; he was admired as a Professor. He explained the Holy Scriptures with a mavellous clearness. He was a subtle Philosopher, a profound Theologian. In controversy he was so powerful that he was called the hammer of heretics. In a word, it is said he knew all that could be known.

With all this knowledge there was one thing that he did not know, namely, his own weakness. Puffed up with science, he had a high opinion of himself, and though he had spoken many things well of God, he had not reached the proper sentiments of His greatness. He did not comprehend that God is incomprehensible; that it is not possible for the feeble mind of man to sound the

abysses of His nature, or to explain by human
words mysteries that are impenetrable. God, who
regarded him with the eye of His compassion,
would not leave him in that blindness, which was
in a measure the punishment of the pride of his
heart. He opened his eyes in a way that brought
him low, and covered him with confusion, a shame
of more profit to him than all the knowledge he
had acquired with so much pain through the
space of many years.

One day Alan had the thought to let it be seen
to what length his knowledge in matters of theology extended. He gave notice that he would explain and give a full knowledge to his hearers
of all the profound mystéries of the holy and
adorable Trinity. As he walked along the river's
side, thinking with himself how he should acquit
himself of his promise, he found a child holding in
its hand a spoon, and taking with it water out of
the river, which it cast into a little hole in the
sand, where it immediately sank through. Alan,
after watching the child awhile, said to it, " What
are you doing there ?" The child answered, "I
have resolved to put all the water of the river into
this hole, and I shall not stop till I have done it."
Alan said, "How long will you take to do it ?
why, it is impossible, my child." "I shall accomplish it sooner than you will what you have
got in your mind," replied the child. "And what
have I in my mind ?" said Alan. "You have it
in your mind," said the child, "to explain the

mysteries of the Holy Trinity, and that, with all
your knowledge, is more impossible to do than for
me to empty the river into this hole."

This answer pierced the heart of Alan, and filled
it with fear and amazement. Being returned home,
he reflected deeply on the words of the child,
whom he knew to be more than a child, and being
touched with lively sentiments of grief at the presumption and vanity of his thoughts, he resolved
not to treat of the mystery at all, but to give himself to the Trinity by a true conversion of heart.
Having mounted into the pulpit the next day, he
said but a few words, despising the shame he
might draw upon himself for not fulfilling his promise.   He then left Paris, and made a sacrifice of
all his knowledge, becoming a Convert Brother in
the Monastery of Citeaux.

It is said he disputed with a heretic in the
Council of Lateran, having obtained permission
from his Abbot for this purpose.   This, however,
seems very uncertain.   He lived unknown and un-
noticed, but, at his death, which took place in the
year of grace 1270, he was buried in great
honour with S. Stephen and the other Abbots of
Citeaux.

LIFE OF THE BLESSED CHRISTIAN,

MONK OF HEISTERBACH.

THE Blessed Christian had, when a young man, pursued a wild course, but the Lord having touched his heart, he fled into the Monastery of Heisterbach, of the Order of Citeaux, in the diocese of Cologne. He was afflicted by God with a number of infirmities, especially with great pains in his head, which were almost continual. One day, when at prayer after the Vigils, near one of the Altars, he rested his head a little for pain, and fell asleep. Scarcely was he asleep when an invisible hand struck him rudely, and he heard a voice saying, "Christian, this is not the place for sleep, but for prayer." From that time forth he was very diligent in his prayer.

He had permission, on account of the pains in his head, to be absent from the Vigils of the night; but scarce ever did he use this permission. Upon this the Abbot Henry said to him : "You complain so much of your pains, and yet you will not use the permission I have given you to be absent from the Quire." The holy man replied: "When I am not in Choir and I hear the Brethren chanting the praises of God, I feel sad, because I remember the consolation my soul has been filled with when I have been at the Choir with my Brethren." Henry having pressed him to say what consolations, he answered that he often saw the Angels, and sometimes our Lord Jesus Christ Himself, in the Choir with the Monks.

The holy man had a particular gift of tears from the Almighty God. This gift having been at one time withdrawn, he felt that if he only might kiss the relic of the true cross which was in the Monastery, he should have this gift restored to him. Being permitted to do so, he was not disappointed of his hope.

On Saint Agatha's day, in the year of grace 1201, this patient Brother, purified by his pains, went to receive his reward.

LIFE OF

BLESSED BERNARD OF ESCOBAR,

ABBOT OF MOUNT SION.

THE Blessed Bernard of Escobar was a native of Toledo, small of stature, but of great learning, being a doctor of Canon law, and celebrated as a Theologian, as well as a famous Hebrew scholar. Of gentle disposition, he made himself dear to all, and embracing the Monastic life in the Monastery of Mount Sion, he breathed forth the sweet odour of virtues, becoming a comfort and support to his Brethren.

His very look mirrored forth the perfection and purity of his holy soul, and at the death of the Abbot he was chosen with one consent to the rule of the flock of Christ.

In that Monastery were two Brethren, who, forgetful of their high profession, led a life of sloth and languor, in which indeed one far exceeded the other. The Blessed Bernard did what he could to bring them to a better way, but all in vain, so that death surprised them in this lukewarm state. About eight years after their death, whilst the holy Abbot sat at his table in his own cell, one of these Brethren, entering the door of the cell, with a countenance moderately cheerful, but

5

having on it a shade of sadness, came forward
towards the Abbot, and bowing to him profoundly, retired to a certain recess in the chamber,
without saying a word. The Abbot was amazed,
not knowing what it was the spirit desired of him,
except that he could not doubt he expected some
assistance at his hands. Whilst these thoughts
passed rapidly through his mind, he beheld the
second Monk enter by the same door as the
other. This last Brother had a very sad look, his
hood was drawn down over his head, and his
eyes and whole face were bathed in tears, and
from his manner of walking it was plain what
great pains he was suffering. The Abbot regarded
him attentively, and knew that it was the same
Brother who, whilst on earth, had so negligently
fulfilled the duties of his profession. He passed
the Abbot like the first one, but without bowing,
and entered the same recess as the other. The
venerable old man, supposing that they waited
there to signify something to him, himself entered
the recess, but found no one. Seeing therefore
that by this mute language the departed Brothers
would let him know of their distress, he offered
for them the holy Sacrifice of the Mass, and added
prayer upon prayer for their liberation, not doubting that the most high God would have respect to
his offering in their behalf.

As the Blessed man increased in years, the
labour and burden of the Choir duties became
intolerable to him, and he was sent to the Monas-

tery of Bonnevaux, which is dependent on that of Mount Sion, and there in solitude, free from every care, he gave himself entirely to contemplation and to prayer, waiting and longing for the happy hour of his release from the burden of the flesh. As he saw death approaching, he grew the more instant in prayer, that with all pureness his soul might ascend to the bridal chamber of the great King. On the day before he passed, he rose from his bed, and with the assistance of one of the Brethren entered the Church, and assisting at the holy Sacrifice in the Chapel of S. Bernard, received there the most sacred Body of the Lord. The next day he died, in the year of our Lord 1606.

Shortly after his death his soul appeared in great glory to a Brother named Justus, of the same Monastery. This Brother had been taken sick on the same day on which the venerable Bernard had passed away. The sick man asked the apparition who or what he was. The spirit replied: "I am the soul of Bernard." He then signified to him to prepare for death, for that he was shortly to be called away from this earth. The next day therefore the sick Brother sent for the Prior, and relating to him the vision, and receiving the last sacraments of religion, he expired towards sundown on the Eve of Lady Day, giving up his spirit to God with great joy of heart.

LIFE OF BLESSED BONIFACE,

BISHOP OF LAUSANNE.

BLESSED Boniface was born at Brussels, of decent and religious parents. His mother, whilst pregnant, was hastening, with her wonted piety, to mattins, when she was met by a venerable man with hair white as snow, and of an angelic countenance, who said to her, "Thou hast within thee one who will be great, and beloved by God and men," and with these words he vanished. When the child was brought forth, she called him Boniface. Exceedingly chaste he was from his infancy, and even if his mother, or grandmother, or his nurse, kissed him, he immediately wiped the kiss away with his clothing, or washed it off his mouth with water.

When five years old he began to study, and made rapid progress till at the age of seventeen he went to the University of Paris. He was there made Doctor of Theology, and for seven years gave lectures publicly. He lived at Paris thirty years. When he celebrated Mass, for he had been made a priest, so greatly was his heart affected, that his face was always wet with weeping. He wore a shirt of horse-hair to tame the rebellious flesh. The Blessed Virgin, to whom he had a singular devotion, appeared to him once when he was afflicted with sickness, and he cried out, "O, Blessed Lady, sanctify me." She answered, "I have sanctified thee, and I will yet again sanctify thee." From Paris he went to Cologne, where he also publicly taught in the schools. It was when there that he was elected Bishop of Lausanne. He reluctantly accepted this post. The church was filled with the wicked. Even the clergy, despising all rule, lived in the most disorderly fashion, so that many who daily offered, or should offer, the Immaculate Victim, were not ashamed publicly to marry and live with wives, as though it were lawful for them so to do. The holy Bishop spoke plainly in his sermons against this detestable vice. These sons of Belial, therefore, conspired against him to kill him. He was celebrating the sacred Mysteries, when they came in with a tumult to slay him before the altar. But, a Franciscan Brother becoming aware of it, raised his voice like a trumpet, and the whole city being moved, came together to the relief of their pastor. The Bishop soon afterwards went to Rome and begged to resign the charge committed to him. Not being able to obtain his request, he remained a whole year at Rome, till the Supreme Pontiff at last consented, begging him, however, to accept some other bishopric. This he would in no wise consent to, saying that he was too worn out and unfit for the work. He begged rather to be allowed to retire to some Monastery, and, obtaining leave, he returned to his own country. Here, going on a visit to a convent called the Chamber of Blessed Mary, one of the Nuns said to him, "It is the will of the Holy Virgin and of her Son, that you should pass the rest of your days in this place." He gladly consented, and soon after received there the Cistercian habit. He attained such perfection that God was pleased to work miracles by his hands.

There was a certain Cardinal sick at Paris, and shortly expecting his end, when one night the Blessed Boniface appeared to him in a vision, surrounded with a glorious light. There came in with him a most beautiful Virgin adorned with jewels. The Bishop was clad also in his Pontifical dress. Addressing the sick man, he asked him how he was. The Cardinal replied, "I am very weak." The holy Bishop signed his forehead, and passed his hand over his face and breast, and at once the sick man felt quite cured. Then he asked, "Who is that young maiden you bring with you?" to which the Bishop answered, "It is S. Agnes," and at once disappeared from his view.

Now, it happened that in the Chamber of Blessed Mary, a certain servant became sick even to death, but his tongue was tied by the devil so that he could not confess. Many priests had tried to draw from him the confession of his sins, but were unable. At last, the man of God was sent for. He told the sick man to confess his sins.

The man replied he would willingly do so if he could. The Bishop told a priest who was present to bring the Holy Sacrament, which he accordingly did. "Dost thou believe," said the Bishop to the sick man, "that this is the Body of Christ, and that He is thy salvation and Deliverance?" He replied, "I believe." The Bishop said to the priest, "Give him the Body of the Lord." He did so, and immediately the sick man was delivered, made at once his confession, and died immediately after.

When William, king of Germany, was besieging a certain city, the holy Bishop was at prayer in the Chamber of Blessed Mary, and he saw in the spirit an armed soldier, clad in white armour, sitting on a white horse, with a lance in his hand, and followed by other soldiers. And whilst the Bishop wondered who it was, and whither he was going, he received an answer to his thoughts from an angel of God. "This is S. George, whom the Lord has sent to aid King William, he will bring the king into the city;" and so it fell out, for that day the king gained the victory.

The holy man grieved much for the soul of Aristotle, and often prayed that, if it were possible, he might find mercy, when there came a voice from heaven, saying, "Pray not for his soul any more, for he did not found my Church, like Peter and Paul, nor did he teach my law."

On the Octave of S. John Baptist's Day, intent on the contemplation of heavenly things, in his meditation the fire of love began to consume him, and a great desire of consolation from on high took hold of him; when, lo! the Queen of heaven, having a crown on her head, and with her a band of Virgins clad in bright array, came to visit him. They sat on one side of the bed, and on the other sat S. John Baptist, giving, by their delightful presence, the most sweet consolation to the holy man. They remained with him a good part of the night, and all disappeared together. Another time, when Boniface was bewailing the sins of his youth, with a sorrow that could not be comforted, there appeared before him two beautiful Virgins, one of whom held a scroll in her hand. She gave it to him, and said, "Read what is contained in this."—"I cannot read anything, for no letters appear to be on it," he replied. "So," said she, "are all thy sins blotted out in the sight of the Lord thy God," saying which she disappeared.

When the old man had become very feeble, he still offered in the Sacrifice of the Mass the peace-making Victim, and a holy Nun saw one day two Angels, one on the right hand and another on the left, holding up the arms of the Priest of God, which for very weakness he was unable to do unaided. They also assisted him in all his other movements, shewing the greatest reverence for him by their gestures.

Once when he could not rise for the Vigils with the rest, as he lay on his bed sorrowful, he complained to the most holy Virgin of his loneliness, when immediately this pitiful Mother came, bearing in her arms the Desired of all nations, wrapped in swaddling clothes, and laid Him on the bed. The Infant, drawing one hand out from the swaddling bands, raised the cloth from His face, as it were to let the holy Boniface gaze on His beauty. Boniface, ravished with its comeliness, cried out: "If in Paradise there were nothing else but that Blessed Face, it were worth while to suffer all tribulations, that we might gaze on a countenance so glorious."

Whilst he continued his prayers he was rapt in the spirit, and was led into Paradise, and saw the Cherubim how they burn and are inflamed. Afterwards he was led into each choir of Angels, and into that of the Prophets, and saw their dignities. Then the glory of the Apostles and founders of the Churches was unfolded before him. Then he came to the choirs of the Martyrs strong in war, and in their blood, and he saw their glory. Afterwards he came to the choirs of the Confessors, who bore up the Church of God by word and example, and he contemplated their glory. Then he came to the choir of Virgins, who follow the Lamb whithersoever He goeth. He beheld their dignity, enraptured with their splendour and beauty. Then he beheld the glory of the ever-blessed Virgin Mary, with what reverence she is honoured by her Son, and by all the Saints, and at the last he came before the Majesty of God, where he saw the Son in the Father, and the

Father in the Son, and the Holy Ghost proceeding from both, and how God is in His Saints. But of that glory and union and dignity, it is better to be silent with reverence, than to say anything, for whatever can be said is nothing compared with the reality. When he returned to himself, and afterwards spoke with the Monks and Nuns of the heavenly home, he seemed to melt with devotion and divine grace, as wax melts at the presence of the fire.

After this vision he fell into a great sickness, nevertheless he every day celebrated the sacred Mysteries, weak and feeble though he was. At last his bodily strength wholly left him, and on February 19th, about the year 1260, he was translated to a better world, full of days, being about seventy-eight years old.

The remains of the Blessed man were laid in a tomb in the choir of the Church of S. John Baptist. On the day of his death a distribution of bread was made every year for a long time, on account of the many benefits he bestowed on the Monastery. The loaves got the name of the loaves of S. Boniface. The time of distribution was afterwards changed to *Lætare* Sunday.

During the time of the civil wars in Belgium the Monastery was burnt down, and the Nuns dispersed. On their return they put the buildings in repair except the Church, which was wholly destroyed. In 1660 the Abbess determined to translate the bones of the holy man to some more honourable place. It was pretty well known where the body had been deposited. They began the search on the second of June, 1660, and on the next day they found the entire skeleton, all else being decayed into dust.

Several miraculous cures were wrought by the application of the holy relics to different persons, and a sweet odour was observed to come from the place where the body had rested.

A rumour of the elevation of the body of the Blessed Boniface, without the sanction of the Ordinary, having reached the ears of the Archbishop of Mechlin, he forbade any veneration to be paid to it, till he had certified himself, first that it was really the body of Boniface, and secondly that he had died in the odour of sanctity. After making the necessary inquest, he decreed that the relics which had been publicly venerated, whilst concealed, might be publicly exposed for veneration in a shrine, near the altar, but that the honour given to them must not be such as is given to a Canonised Saint.

Such was the decree of the Archbishop, for the honour given to a Canonised Saint differs from that given to a Saint not Canonised. Canonised Saints may be publicly invoked in the Litanies and common prayers of the Church ; Churches and Altars may be set up in their honour. Festivals with the Mass and Canonical hours may be celebrated in their memory. A Saint not Canonised may be publicly venerated, but his name cannot be introduced into Church prayers or litanies. His relics also may be honoured with flowers, lights, carpeting, &c., but not by any Church function. He may be venerated by the kissing of his relics, and by invocation in private prayers, made even in the hearing of others.

It may seem strange that Boniface received the Monastic habit in a Monastery of Nuns, but it is found that frequently cases of the same sort have occurred in the annals of the Cistercian Order. The Cell of the holy man was, however, some little distance from the Convent, and has since been made into a Chapel.

LIFE OF

BLESSED PETER OF TOULOUSE,

MONK OF CLAIRVAULX.

THE Blessed Peter, before he left the world, being anxious to know what he might do to be saved, had a vision. He saw the Lord sitting on a throne, high and elevated. Before Him were ten thousands of His Saints. Then Peter was brought before the judgment seat. At the terrible majesty of the Judge his heart fainted for fear, and casting himself at His feet he begged Him to have pity on him. The Lord answered him: "What will you that I should do for you?" Peter replied: "Lord, that I may be saved." The Lord answered: "Be converted to Me without delay, and persevere in My service till death, and you shall enjoy the happiness you desire."

Peter, having received this promise, and looking upon it as a sure earnest of salvation, renounced the world, and gave himself wholly to the service of God. He was yet a young man when he withdrew into the desert, afflicting his soul with fasting, and offering to God daily the sacrifice of a broken and contrite spirit. His meat was nothing but wild herbs, and a bad kind of bread. The devil attacked him with a thousand different temptations, but was unable to overcome him in one.

The marvels wrought by the most holy Father Bernard reached the ears of the hermit Peter, and in A.D. 1144 he resolved to seek the shelter of Clairvaulx, hoping there to be more free from the attacks of the evil one, and to enjoy the guidance of so great a pastor.

God's thoughts are not as our thoughts, and by His permission the man of God was tormented by the devil at Clairvaulx with far more violence than he had been in the desert. Night or day he gave him no rest, and all the rudest penitences were of no avail to drive him away.

Once he appeared to him in the Choir like a horrible giant, his eyes casting forth flames of fire. He darted at Peter a terrible look, which as it were bound him to the spot, so that he lost all power of motion. At length the Lord came to his assistance, and when he had made the sign of the cross, his discomfited foe disappeared. He appeared another time as a hideous monster, which seemed about to leap on the man of God to devour him. He called upon the Lord for help, and the evil beast fled away.

One night he had a vision. The Angel of the Lord appeared to him under the guise of a physician, and told him that if he would submit to the pain he would put an end to his temptations. He consented willingly. It then seemed as if the physician performed some operation upon him,

which put him to great pain. He awoke full of
consolation and a sweet peace of soul, which ever
afterwards remained with him, so that he could
say to God with the Psalmist, " According to the
troubles that I had in my heart Thy comforts
have refreshed my soul." The holy man now
tasted how sweet the Lord is, and his tenderness
of heart was manifested by the abundance of tears
which he shed continually, but especially when he
offered the Adorable Sacrifice. The Lord also
revealed many things to His servant, touching the
joys of the Blessed, giving him sometimes such a
foretaste of the good things of the world to come,
that he was ravished out of himself.

One day, as he held the Sacred Host in his
hands, at the time he was about to make his
Communion, of a sudden he beheld, not the Host,
but in its stead a Child of ravishing beauty. The
sight filled him with respectful fear, and not
daring to give his eyes the liberty to look on such
Majesty, he closed them, all dazzled as they were
with the brightness of the glory. But He whose
delight is to be with the children of men, though
his eyes were perfectly close, still appeared to
him as clearly as if they had been wide open.
Nor could he turn his eyes away from the sight of
that glory, for the Lord as. it were held his gaze
fixed on Himself, filling his soul at the same
time with an inexpressible sweetness. This took
place not once only, but almost every day for the
space of four or five months, so that there was

scarcely a day on which the Lord did not appear to him. Sometimes the grace was not at once given, but the servant of God stood before Him, with such a mixture of respect and confidence, that scarcely ever did he finish the celebration of the Holy Sacrifice without having received the accustomed favour.

These visions he made known to one of the Monks, who with great importunity drew the history of them from him, on the condition that he should not make them known while he lived.

His heart, now wounded with love, had no rest, sighing for the perfect possession of that Beauty, a faint glimpse of which had so charmed his heart.· He desired to drink to the full of that river of pleasure which makes glad the city of God, seeing that a few drops of its waters had inebriated his soul. The Lord hastened to bring him to his eternal rest, and his death took place about A.D. 1167.

LIFE OF BLESSED SIMON,

MONK OF ALNE.

THE Blessed Simon came of rich and noble parentage. From his childhood the grace of God was with him. He passed his earliest years in the pursuit of arms, but when he had attained the age of sixteen, renouncing his fortune, his country, and his parents, he entered the Monastery of Alne, near Liege, with the design of becoming a Convert Brother.

When he had made his profession he was sent to keep the sheep. In this occupation he put before his eyes the Patriarchs of old as his examples. The solitude he enjoyed in this employment carried him towards God, with Whom alone he conversed, far removed from creatures. The Lord God filled him with special lights and graces, discovering to him His secrets as of old to Moses, when he fed his flocks in the desert. He not only gave him lights within his soul, but He gave him also sensible marks of His presence, by a bright light which sometimes appeared in the night, the sight of which filled his heart with vehement flames of love.

The Enemy of mankind did not leave him alone to enjoy the heavenly sweetness, but persecuted

6

the Blessed man with fiendish malice. Sometimes he would clog the movements of his body,
as it were by a heavy weight, almost insupport-
able, oppressing his mind at the same time with
a thick gloom, so that he seemed neither awake
nor asleep. In this state he pressed upon him to
blaspheme the name of God, suggesting to him
the most horrible thoughts. The Blessed man,
however, resisted firmly all these temptations, and
at length the light of God's countenance shining
upon him scattered all the temptations of the
Enemy, establishing his soul in abundance of
peace, and taking away the weight that had oppressed his body.

The spirit of darkness now tried him after
another fashion. He appeared to him in various
hateful forms, sometimes striking him severely
with a rod. Then he appeared to him in a
dream, shewing him a horrible pit filled with
flames, into which he threatened to cast him.
His feet were so burned by the heat, that for
forty days he was compelled to remain in bed, not
being able to stand or walk.

God gave to this Brother the knowledge of the
secrets of the heart. To some persons the
Blessed man revealed their past sins, exhorting
them to a change of life. His name became so
celebrated in France and Italy by his gift of prophecy, that Pope Innocent III. sent for him in
A.D. 1216, to be present at the Council of Lateran.

Another Convert Brother, who was opposite to

him in Choir, having during the Office thought within himself that Simon was no better than others, and that his prophecies were but conjectures, the holy man afterwards, to his great astonishment, discovered to him that he knew his thoughts, telling him for the future to be charitable in his judgments.

The holy man went to receive his crown in the year of Redemption 1228.

OF SAINT ISEMBERG,

OF HEMMENRODE.

THE Blessed Isemberg had passed thirty years in the Abbey of Hemmenrode when his earthly pilgrimage was ended.

Those who waited on him in the Infirmary, seeing his lips move one midnight, thought perhaps he was wandering, but on listening with their ears to his mouth, they were surprised at the beautiful words which they heard him uttering about God and the joys of heaven. They immediately let the Abbot know, who, though he himself was not well, yet came at once to the chamber.

As soon as Isemberg saw him, he said to him: "Oh what an agreeable night I have passed, Reverend Father. What a beautiful harmony I have heard! I was up this night in the choirs of the Saints, singing the praises of God. O how melodious is their chant! and how well their voices accord one with another. Those who sing on earth become weary, and their voices often agree not one with another. But above it is far different, and without pain or weariness they praise God without end. The more they praise Him the greater is their desire to sing His praises still, and their only rest and repose is His unceasing praise, which in an inexpressible manner satisfies their souls. I saw some of the Monks of our Order, with a glory greatly excelling that of others. For in proportion as they have humbled and abased themselves on earth, so is their glory and elevation in heaven. I talked with many of our Brethren, who were clad in white raiment, so white that my eyes could not endure the glorious brightness. I asked them if it should be given to me to be clothed in garments white as those. They answered me that he, who would be so clothed, must walk unblamably and without spot before the Lord."

When he had got as far as these words he became so weak that he could speak no more. They gave him therefore a little water, and having paused awhile he went on to say, "I wish God may leave me my life till the Office is over, that I might speak to my Lords, that is to the Brethren, for I have things so comforting to tell them, about the unutterable good things which God has prepared for them that love Him, and that devoutly sing His praises." The Abbot said to him: "What did you see, Brother?" He answered: "I was taken up this night into heaven, and I saw the great Queen of Heaven our Lady, who promised to be with me. And I saw Michael the Archangel, whose protection I have ever devoutly sought, and a great host of Angels ready to assist me."

He again stopped through utter feebleness, and the Abbot bade him take something to ease the dryness of his throat. He then cried out: "O how sweet is the Lord to those that taste and see! How great, how inexpressibly delicious the sweetness He has made me to experience this night! How far it exceeds all thought of man! How greatly desirable and much to be longed for! I taste it in the heart, but cannot express it by the mouth. This heavenly meat fills my soul with such unutterable sweetness as to take away all relish for everything earthly. Earthly nourishment gives but a passing solace, but this feeds and satisfies the soul for all eternity. O how happy are those Blessed ones, who shall enjoy it in heaven for ever and for ever."

The Abbot then brought two Novices, who had been brave warriors in the world, into the chamber of the Blessed man. Isemberg, seeing them, said: "You are truly happy in having received grace from God to escape from the snares of the world, in which you were once taken. You have now an assured salvation, if you follow on to the end the course you have happily begun, and will enjoy those inconceivably good things which God hath in reserve for His faithful ones." Then, naming one of them, he said that, had he not entered the Monastery, he would without doubt have perished everlastingly.

The Abbot then sent for two persons, who were staying in the apartments allotted to guests, that hearing the words of the Blessed man, they might be converted. At first they refused to come, being much attached to the world. At last they came, and told him how they wished to leave the world, but had not the courage. They asked him to pray for them. " Ah !" he said, " if God had showed you what I have seen, you would utterly despise all worldly glory." After they had asked him some questions, and he had answered in such manner, as that it was plain he read the secrets of the heart and conscience, he was quite exhausted, and rendered up his soul into the arms of his Saviour, to go and drink of that torrent of pleasure to the full, of which he had received such a foretaste here below.

He passed from earth about the year 1180.

LIFE OF THE VENERABLE ARNULPH,

ARNULPH of Gestele was tenth Abbot of Villers. When yet a young man, he would not go to study at Paris, desiring rather that charity which edifieth, than knowledge which puffeth up. Imitating, therefore, the example of the holy Father Benedict, he neglected the learning of the world, and gave himself altogether to religion. The fame of his virtues spread abroad, and the Monks of St. Bernard's Place, near Antwerp, chose him for their Abbot.

When he had undertaken this charge, he took care not to pull down by his actions what he taught by his words. Whilst engaged in his work he was elected Abbot of Villers, but he refused to accept the care of so large a Monastery. Now, according to the statutes of the Order, one who will not be Abbot at the Mother house, may not be Abbot of any house, which it has founded. Accordingly, the Blessed Arnulph ceased to govern his Abbey, but instructed the Brethren only by his presence. There is no wisdom, however, against the Lord. The Abbot elected at Villers died no long time after, and again the Brethren chose Arnulph, who, no longer kicking against the goad, consented to the election, as being the ordinance of God.

He found the Abbey loaded with debts, and obliged to several payments, so that, in the first year of his rule, the Brethren never tasted wine in the Refectory. But he, remembering what is said in the Gospel, "Seek ye first the kingdom of heaven, and His justice, and all these things shall be added to you;" paying little attention to the want of worldly substance, took care rather of the souls committed to his governance. He brought back to the Cloister those Choir-monks whom he found staying long at the Granges, according to the statute of the ancient uses, " The Cloister ought to be the dwelling-place of the Choir Brothers. They may go to the Granges, but it is not advisable that they should continue long there." He further said that the office of Choir Brothers is to pray, read, sing, meditate, handle the flesh of the Immaculate Lamb, and keep themselves unspotted from the world; that it is not suitable to their profession to be engaged in rural work, philosophic study, lawsuits, slumber, talking, gluttony, &c., especially where external matters can be performed either by Convert Brothers, or faithful secular persons. The Spirit of truth, which inspired him with this judgment, did not deceive him, but, by the help of God, and the industry of the Convert Brothers, the house was relieved from debts, increased in substance and good buildings.

The holy Abbot showed himself an example of

sobriety, content to live as the rest of his community in food and clothing. When those in Office,
as the custom was, came to ask permission of him
to give and receive in the matters of their admin-
istration, he used to say, "You must know,
Brothers, that I myself who am the chief steward
of the temporal things, cannot give away a single
loaf, unless either it be for the service of the
Monastery, or the relief of the poor, to whom the
goods belong."

This faithful steward affirmed that never, during
the time of his holding the office of Abbot, had he
gone out of the Monastery for other ends than the
affairs of the Order, or of his own house.

Fearing to spend idly the patrimony of the
Crucified, he showed himself a pattern of humility,
whether walking or riding. When he made his
visitations, he took with him but two couriers, a
Choir Brother for secretary, and a Convert Brother,
being no burden upon the Monasteries. He was
much loved for his humility by the Duke of
Brabant, by the people, and especially by the
Convert Brothers. Of these latter he increased
the number of their garments, compassionating
their want of clothing. He received many Convert Brothers to Religion, saying that he had no
right to reject labourers, who were truly penitent,
from Religion ; that the Order had been founded
for this very end, that unlettered laymen, as well
as learned persons, might find in it a refuge from
the trammels and snares of the devil. His Monas-

tery became very large, and he had at the same time one hundred Monks in the choir, and three hundred Convert Brothers. He used himself to go round their choir during the Vigils, to see that they were wakeful, and when he found many there, his heart was gladdened with their devotion.

In the last year of his life, when the visitation was over, he gave permission to the Community, that after the number of clothes had been increased, the whole of the goods of the Monastery should be applied for the needs of the Refectory. The debts of the Abbey were now all paid, and, having been Abbot five years, he departed to the Lord, March 2nd, A.D. 1276.

LIFE OF THE BLESSED PONTIUS,

BISHOP OF CLAREMONT.

THE Servant of Christ, Pontius, was a Monk of Grandselve, in the diocese of Toulouse. Amongst a number of venerable Brethren, who excelled in the gifts and graces of the Holy Spirit, he sought by all means to crucify himself to the world, having only for his friends those ancients who were eminent for their religion. Sighing with desire after the heavenly country, he eagerly sought their acquaintance, that, strengthened by their example and exhortations, he might be renewed day by day in the spirit of his mind, and profiting by this daily increase, ascend to the knowledge of true wisdom.

There was one to whom, even more than to the rest, his soul was united with a special attachment of love. He was the Master of the Novices, deeply rooted in every virtue, and a most pure holiness of life. This old man thought of nothing but of that rest of everlasting gladness which he hoped for as in some sort the recompense of his long labours. The things of the world and the flesh brought no delight to him, for his inmost heart panted for nothing else but the blessed presence of our Lord Christ; to

be dissolved, and to be with Him. At the time
of this agony of spiritual desire, as he daily said,
"When shall I come to appear before the presence of God," the day of the Supper of the Lord
came on, when the whole company of the
Brethren approaches the Table of the Lord to
partake of the life-giving Sacraments. When at
the hour of the Divine Sacrifice they drew near,
each in his order, to Communion, he also went
amongst the rest to be partaker of the Divine
Gift. Having received the Sacred Communion,
and whilst the health-giving Eucharist was still
retained in his mouth, his soul melted away for
the very sweetness of the divine love, and with
the fervour of sacred desire he sought for his soul
that he might die, pouring forth to the Lord this
manner of prayer.

"O Lord Jesus Christ, Son of the Living God,
Saviour of mankind, Who this most innocent
Flesh, which I unworthy have presumed to receive, didst take of the womb of a Virgin, undefiled and without spot, for us sinners; if this the
petition of Thy poor servant do not displease
Thee, I beseech Thy kind clemency that never
again Thou wouldst permit any earthly food to go
through this passage of my throat by which I am
about to swallow now the Bread of heaven."

Saying these words, he then consumed the
Sacred Host which was still in his mouth, receiving it rather into his inmost soul than into
his body.

It seemed as if the Lord at once answered, "As thou hast asked, so be it done to thee." At that very hour his bodily strength began to fail, and on the third day, that is, on the Holy Saturday of the Pasch, he slept sweetly in the Lord. He went to be eternally satisfied with the sight of that Face into which the Angels desire to look, and which he had sought with so many sighs and wishes. Blessed man, so to receive the fulfilment of his heart's desire! happy prayer, which so speedily ran to its accomplishment! Blessed Pontius, who with every care tended the sick and dying man, asked him if he felt any pain to trouble him. He replied, "No, unless a little in his throat, just where he had placed his finger when making his prayer." Pontius, full of holy delight to see one dying so happily, asked of him, if by the divine permission it might be, that he would return to him and let him know something of his state beyond the grave. A few days after he had entered into his rest, he appeared to Pontius, shining with great glory, and all translucent, like crystal or the most pure glass. "My beloved one," he said, "know that by the mercy of the Lord I have been received to greatest blessedness. This body, however, in which you see me, is lent me till the day of the general resurrection. At that day I shall recover my own body, which at the present has become the food of worms, and is turned again into dust; and the body of my resurrection will be beyond all com-

parison more excellent and more glorious than
that in which I at present am manifest. Meantime, I now rest in this, which is in all things
convenient to me, and so translucid that I can
see from all its parts and members as clearly as if
my whole body were one eye."

But in one foot of this most pure body appeared the spot of a certain dark obscurity, at
which as he spoke he cast a somewhat sorrowful
glance. "That spot," said he, "which you
behold, is the fruit of my negligence, because,
when the Brethren went out to the daily labour, I
walked sometimes sluggishly, and did not follow
them with the fervour I ought to have had." This
and many other things this holy soul said to the
Blessed Pontius, and at length retiring left him
marvellously edified and consoled. As however it
is certain that all will appear before the throne of
God without spot or wrinkle or any such thing, it
must by no means be believed that this Saint still
retained any stain in the heavenly court, or that
his spirit was contained in a body transparent as
crystal. But these things, for the correction and
instruction of manners, are, by the permission of
God, made manifest to men in visible appear-
ances. They are, however, to be piously explained, and are not to be taken according to the
letter.

This vision the servant of Christ Pontius was
found worthy to behold for the consolation of
those who in the Cistercian Order bear the burden

and heat of the day. As time went on he was called himself, on account of his virtue and deserts, to the government of this same Abbey of Grandselve. He adorned with worthy behaviour the place of honour, exercising the pastor's care with due authority, yet not losing the meekness and simplicity of a sheep. In the days when he was ruler of the flock, the Lord, by a hidden counsel of His tremendous judgments, sent the steps of a fearful mortality walking through the house. Within the space of two months forty-five Brethren were taken out of their midst. They fell asleep with such eagerness of pious desire, that it was as if they had known beforehand from heaven the surety of their participation in the blessedness of life eternal, as soon as the miseries of this earthly course should be over.

Many really did foresee that this heavenly grace should be bestowed upon them. Out of these many cases it will be enough to relate one, for example's sake.

There was a Monk of approved conversation, who died in the mortality just spoken of. Having come to his last hour the tablet was beaten after Compline, and the Brothers came together to fortify him for his end. As the Choir sang around him the Litany and Psalms, he himself being strengthened in the Lord, sang as he could with the rest. The psalmody being finished, the Abbot Pontius made a signal to the Brethren to retire, for he saw the sick man joining in the

Psalms, and thought therefore that he would still live some time longer. The Brother, however, seeing this, stretched forth his hand, and signified to the Abbot to make them wait yet a little while, for he knew that he was at the point of departure.

The Abbot could hardly contain himself for joy, seeing that this most fervent man, though at the point of death, would not break silence after Compline, so careful was he of the discipline of the Rule. The Abbot however himself, having first said "Benedicite," spoke to the dying Brother as follows : " Tell us, dearest Brother, for I see that the Lord is with thee, is there anything revealed to thee of that blessed hope which thou waitest for, that we may be able to take comfort in the Lord, and to rejoice with thee ?" Then the sick man replied : " To answer in few words, Reverend Father, to what you ask of me, know that I have seen what it is not lawful to utter. This one thing I can say, that if I alone had more merits than all the race of man put together, I should still be unworthy to obtain the glory of that everlasting blessedness which has been prepared for me, and which has been shown to me now about to depart." Having ended these words he slept in the Lord.

In this same Cloister dwelt a Brother of great religion named Bernard. This Brother, in the beginning of his conversion, whilst he considered the enormity of his offences, and the strict justice of the Sovereign Judge, was moved with such

7

fear as almost to fall into despair. The Abbot
Pontius having been made aware of this, by many
examples and instructions endeavoured to persuade him that, however guilty he might have
been, yet now having repented and confessed, he
would never be deprived of pardon. Still unable
to satisfy his mind, he added, " I give my own
soul in bond for your salvation, so that, if persevering in the Order and obeying its Rules, your
soul should be lost, let my soul be required in its
place." The Brother felt so wonderfully strengthened by hearing this promise, that he entirely put
away the discouraging thoughts that assailed him,
and rejoicing in the Lord with trembling, from
thenceforward began to sing of His mercy and
judgment. Being of noble birth, he esteemed no
nobility but the becoming poor for Christ's sake,
and serving the poor; for he waited on the sick in
the hospital of the poor with a loving service, not
as to strangers and beggars, but as to his masters,
the members of Jesus Christ and sons of God.
If he saw amongst them any one diseased, or full
of sores, or covered with worms, on such a one he
bestowed all his most tender care, washing and
wiping him, and fomenting him as a mother
would the sick child of her womb. He also was
one of those who, whilst employed in this minis-
try, was taken to the Lord in the mortality above
spoken of. As he beheld his companions one by
one as the days advanced going off, he too desired
with great desire to be dissolved and to be with

Christ. The good God, who is ever present with His servants, who are of a contrite heart and of a troubled spirit, determined to fulfil his desire. Having taken a little fever, he began to be sick somewhat, and took to his bed. The Abbot came to visit him in his bed, wondering at the same time that so fervent a Brother, on so slight an illness, should be keeping his bed. He said therefore to him, smiling, "Ah, Brother Bernard, you are not going to die yet; do not be afraid, you will come again to eat a dinner of beans and herbs with us." The Brother however answered, "I am not afraid, Father, but I have confidence in the Lord that I shall not be defrauded of my desire." After four or five days this little spark of a fever had kindled into a great fire. Pontius then laying aside his own thought, saw that what the Brother had said would come to pass. When near the hour of his departure he was anointed with the sacred unction, and seemed of a sudden to be rapt in spirit, lying for a long time without motion or feeling, so that he almost seemed like one dead. Meantime, the heavens were opened to him, and he saw with unveiled face the glory of God, so that he might say, "I have seen the Lord face to face, and my life is preserved." During a whole hour, lying as it were without life, not led by presumption, but with grace for his guide, he scanned the secrets of heaven, and when at length he returned to himself, his glad look sufficiently told where he had been. His kind father Pontius approaching, asked how he found himself, to which he answered, "By the goodness of God it is well with me, my lord and father. And now I set you free from your promise, thanking you much on account of your care for me a sinner, for rightly is the promiser set free, when that which has been promised is taken hold of." The Abbot, however, had forgotten all about what he had bound himself to, as answerable for the salvation of the soul of the Brother. The Brother then said to him: "Have you forgotten that you made yourself answerable for the salvation of my soul? I set you free from your bond, being now secure of my salvation, by the mercy of Jesus Christ our Lord." Then the Abbot began to question him closely as to how he could know this thing. The Brother, however, was by no means willing to make known his secret. The Abbot, therefore, seeing that he prevailed nothing by entreaty, commanded him in the name of the Lord, and by virtue of holy obedience, to conceal nothing, but to manifest all for the edification and comfort of many. Upon this the Brother, compelled by obedience, related as follows: "Being no longer permitted to keep silence I will tell you a thing you will perhaps .scarcely believe. However, in order that you may have a proof of the truth of my words, know that as soon as they are finished my life also will come to a close. You must know then that though I am most miserable and

unworthy, I have been presented before our Lord
and Saviour Jesus Christ, and have seen Him
face to face; not indeed in His Godhead, but in
the form of manhood which He vouchsafed for
our sakes to assume. And by His most kind
pardon I have received the remission of all my
sins, and through His grace have the hope of
everlasting blessedness laid up in my bosom.
For from His own most sacred mouth I heard
that all who shall have persevered obedient in this
Order until death, shall obtain eternal life. And
I saw our Brethren who had passed out of
this world glorified with great glory, and I saw
the place amongst them which by the mercy of
the Lord shall be allotted to me." Having ended
these words he gave up the ghost.

See how the kingdom of heaven suffereth violence, and the violent bear it away, according to the
testimony of the Lord. This sinner, who in the
beginning of his conversion dared not look up to
the height of the heavens for the multitude of his
crimes, having now offered to God the sacrifice
of a broken spirit was found worthy not only to
behold the face of the Lord appeased, but even to
see the Lord inviting him to the most excellent
happiness of eternal glory.

During the same mortality, there fell sick
a certain Monk, a Brother whose name was
Stephen. This Brother, from the desire of dying,
would scarcely consent to take any food, sighing
to be released from this workshop of the flesh,

and to be brought out of this exile into the valley
of tears. The Lord gave to him the desire of his
heart. The Brother over the infirmary, who was
continually waiting upon his wants, seeing that he
was dying with such devotion and tranquillity of
soul, was himself taken with the desire to die too.
He said, therefore, to him, "I see, Brother, that
you will soon be delivered from the miseries of
this world, and be introduced into the joy of your
Lord, wherefore I beseech you, when you have come
into the most sweet presence of our Lord Jesus
Christ, ask Him to grant me also, of His gracious
goodness, a speedy release from this world." The
dying Brother promised he would do what he
could. A few days after his falling asleep, he
appeared in a vision to the infirmarian Brother,
and said to him, "Behold, I have been received in peace, and see the good things of the
Lord in the land of the living, which exceed every
delight of flesh and blood. And now, according
to my promise I return to you, not to bring
you the thing you unadvisedly asked, but assistance which I know will be of more advantage to
you. Remember, then, this sin (he here named
a certain sin to the Brother) which you fell into
when in the world, and which requires expiation,
and you have never been absolved from it either
by contrition of heart or confession of the mouth.
Confess, therefore, and do penance with all speed,
for unless it be blotted out before death by confession, after death it will remain for ever unpar-

donable." The Brother, waking from sleep, now clearly remembered the sin which had been committed twelve years before, and had entirely slipped away from his memory. Giving great thanks to God, he hastened to make confession and satisfaction.

In A. D. 1168 Pontius was elected Abbot of Clairvaulx, and thus made a pastor of all the Abbeys founded by this mother house. He did not remain long here, for in A.D. 1172, he was chosen by both clergy and people to be Bishop of Clairmont. He did not, however, lay aside the humility of the Monk because graced with the dignity of the Bishop, but only rendered this dignity more commendable by joining with it the lowliness of the Monastic spirit. He was highly esteemed amongst the Bishops of his time, and employed in the greatest affairs for the welfare of the whole Church. He went to his reward in A.D. 1201.

LIFE OF BLESSED PETER,

ABBOT OF CLAIRVAULX.

THIS man, sprung from the blood of the kings of France, despised all things for the love of Christ, and, making light of his nobility, came to Igni, and there, under the Abbot Guerri, put on the habit of Religion in A. D. 1144. From the beginning of his conversion he lived the life of the perfect. Entire nights he passed in prayer. Watchings, and fastings, and other severities of the Order, he kept with his whole strength and mind, never departing so much as an hair's-breadth from any of the constitutions laid down. All began to look up to him with reverence.

A great lover of chastity, he kept his loins girt, and his lamp burning, by ever having in hand some good work. Knowing that we have this treasure in earthen vessels, he strove ever to keep his body holy and undefiled in sanctification and honour. He delighted in humility, never desiring to be brought forward, but shunning the honour which his good repute procured for him.

He was endued with a most tender piety towards Mary the Mother God, finding no help so powerful against the snares of the wicked one as her protection. Nor did he ever in vain fly to her assistance, but in every encounter with the foe she

ministered to him such a strength as easily gave
him the victory over the Enemy. In all troubles
and difficulties she stood by him, carrying him
through on the straight road of virtue, so that he
neither declined to the right hand or to the left.
His face was always heavenwards, his steps directed
to his everlasting home.

Satan saw it, and enviously sought to turn him
out of the path. Sometimes he would allure him
with the delights of the world, or remind him of
the nobleness of his birth. With this was con-
trasted the severity of the Monastic life, the menial
employments, and constant mortifications. The
holy youth had no other recourse but to fly to his
beloved Mother Mary, looking ever trustfully to
this star of help. One night he was rapt into an
ecstasy, and beheld a beautiful mansion whose
magnificence excelled that of any royal palace.
After gazing with wonder at its outside splendour,
he determined with himself to enter, that he
might behold its perfection within, and learn who
it was that dwelt there. He entered, and, lo! as
it were a spacious kingly hall, adorned with precious stones, and full of glorious light. In the
midst of it was a throne, and on the throne sat a
Queen of a countenance of exceeding beauty and
majesty, whom he at once knew to be the Mother
of God and refuge of sinners. Desiring to approach and salute her, he was about to move forward, when at his first step certain dogs, black
and horrible to behold, ran forward with loud cry

as if to devour him. Full of fear, he dared not
stir, but turned his face in supplication to the
Queen. She, with a voice of authority, drove
away the evil beasts, who, howling, fled out of
sight. Then the Queen bade him to come nigh
without fear, and with her sweet words greatly
consoled the servant of Christ. Such delight did
he enjoy in the glory of her presence, that he
would have wished never to return to the body.
When he was come to himself he lamented with
many tears so great a loss.

This holy man was blessed with a most sweet
and gracious composure, which shone out like a
heavenly light in the continual tranquillity of his
countenance. For, by a divine gift, above the
privilege of nature, he was never ruffled in spirit
by any adverse thing, but always remained in an
untroubled peace. Ever the same gaiety of look,
mixed with a certain modest gravity, was to be
seen in his gentle and courteous face, a look pleasant, yet, at the same time severe. His venerable
Abbot asked him once how it was that he could
always thus remain in the same state. He answered, " When I was a Novice, it seemed to be
as if a certain spirit sensibly took possession of
me, and from then till now this same spirit, or
force, gently rules me, ' leading Joseph like a
sheep.' It collects all my faculties when they
scatter themselves abroad, and when they wish to
apply themselves to other things, it, as it were,
compels them to fix themselves on prayer, some-

times not allowing them to perceive what would naturally strike the ear, or draw the attention of the eye."

One night, on the Lord's day, when the Brethren were in choir, and he with them, a great pain in the head took hold of him. It was presently so grievous that he thought to leave the choir, but, as he began to move from his place, he heard a voice saying to him, "I will call upon the Lord with praise, and so shall I be safe from my enemies." Comforted by this voice, he remained. After a while, the pain continuing, he was again about to go out, when the voice spoke the same words to him, and kept him back. The pain continued till the time of Mass, when, going up in his rank to receive Communion, it seemed, when he bowed forward, as though a huge rock were rolled away from his head, and, after Communion he had no return of his pain.

The blessed man, Peter, though young, was looked up to with confidence by all the Monks in the time of temptation, and they opened to him all the secrets of their hearts, as to an able physician of the soul. A certain Monk being once grievously tormented against faith, asked Peter if he had ever experienced the like temptations. He replied, "I confess freely that I have often been tempted in that sort, but a manifold experience of faith has now put to flight all weakness of that kind." The Monk asked, "What kind of experience?" Peter answered, "I have had much experience of God, and sometimes such as that, when I ceased to have it, I was more sorry for the loss of it than if I had been cast into a burning oven."

As he increased day by day in holiness, and the love of God, he was made Prior of Igni, then in A.D. 1157, Abbot of King's Valley, then Abbot of Igni.

Such grace had he with God, that the most wicked sinners were forgiven at his intercession. There was a certain knight named Baldwin, to whom belonged the castle of Guise, in the diocese of Rheims. This man having not the fear of God before his eyes, was daily engaged in laying waste all within his reach by fire, rapine, and slaughter. One good thing alone was found in him, a sincere love for the Blessed Peter, Abbot of Igni, and for the whole Community. Nor did the Lord leave him unrewarded for this good thing, but dealt with him according to the saying of the Gospel, "He that receiveth a righteous man, in the name of a righteous man, shall receive a righteous man's reward." For, whilst he was of a vigorous age, he was suddenly taken with a mortal sickness. He sent a messenger flying to the holy Abbot, supplicating him to come immediately. The Abbot went with all haste, and found him unable to speak, but, having prayed for him, God vouchsafed to restore to the sick man the power of speech. Having made his confession with a broken and contrite heart, he desired at once to abandon the

world, and to take the habit of Religion. His
wife, however, whilst there yet remained any hope
of his recovery, refused to consent. At last, having lost all hope, she gave way, and he was at
once conveyed to the Abbey, where he received
the habit of Religion, but no time for penance
was given to him, for his soul being loosed from
the body, passed away into the hands of its
Creator.

On the night Baldwin died, he appeared to a
certain Monk, as if lying on a bed pressed with
sickness, and striving to rise. The Monk offered
to help him, but he answered, "Do not trouble
yourself, Brother, for S. Benedict, under whose
wing I have taken refuge, is to me a strong help,
and sends me to the Abbot Peter to be made a
Monk." The same night, when the Abbot was
thinking of the great load of sins committed by
this man, and, going round the altars of the Saints
in spirit to obtain their intercession, he fell into a
sort of state between sleeping and waking. On a
sudden Satan appeared to him with a loud cry of
rage, calling out, "What, will you take Baldwin
from me!" The Evil Beast then leaped forward
upon the Abbot, as if to strangle him. He woke
up, and found, as it were, all his limbs bound.
However, nowise afraid, he said, "I adjure thee,
unclean spirit, by the blood of Jesus Christ shed
for sinners on the cross, and by His glorious Virgin
Mother, not to presume to hurt this penitent
soul." The devil was compelled by this adjura-

tion to depart, leaving his members free, and this relaxing of his limbs he took for a sign of the setting free of the poor sinner.

For thirty days, however, he almost daily offered the Holy Sacrifice for poor Baldwin, asking, in the Chapter, for the prayers of the Brethren. Almost every day Baldwin appeared to him, sometimes when asleep, sometimes when awake, and stood before him, or kneeled with a supplicating look and joined hands, as though beseeching of him not to discontinue his prayers. It happened, during these thirty days, that an Abbot of the Benedictine Order, who had been wronged by Baldwin, came on a visit to Igni. The venerable Peter took occasion to bring this Abbot to Baldwin's grave, where he solemnly absolved him from his offence. On that night Baldwin appeared to the Abbot Peter, showing him that a sore, which had formerly polluted him, was now perfectly healed.

On Good Friday, at the hour at which our Lord and Saviour offered His Blood for sinners, and died the death of the cross, whilst the Abbot was in the church, two young men appeared to him in beautiful apparel. Between them came Baldwin, whom they led up to the altar. As they passed the Abbot, they turned to him and said, "Behold, Sir Baldwin." The Abbot was greatly gladdened at the sight, seeing in this the token of his reconciliation and complete pardon. From this time forth Baldwin appeared no more.

The venerable Abbot was a most watchful shepherd over his sheep, ever considering the account he would have to render of every one of them before the awful judgment seat of God. Each day on the altar he offered the Victim of Peace, to turn away the wrath of the Most High, if by chance any of his sons had sinned. He bewailed the sins of his children as if they were his own, with showers of tears, sighing and sobbing as if his heart would break. By this he had much increased the pains he suffered in his head, and had completely lost the sight of one eye. This loss he rejoiced in, because the eyes are often the windows of sin. Once, speaking to his Monks, he said, "Let us rejoice in the Lord, Brethren, giving Him many thanks. One of my enemies, you see, is dead, though one yet survives. Be assured I would gladly have it perish also, rather than it should cause me to offend in the least point. Much better is it to be without the eyes of the body, and attain to the sight of the eternal glory, than, being possessed of those eyes, to be for ever shut out from the light of the heavenly Jerusalem." This holy man, crucified to the delights of the world, thought but little of what ministered to earthly happiness.

The good Abbot took great care of the sick, sometimes waiting upon them himself, and ministering to them with his own hands, and seeing that everything necessary was supplied to them, to make them regain their bodily strength, and those who were tried with weariness of spirit he comforted with the words of his eloquent tongue.

In receiving men of rank into his monastery, he let them know that superfluity and pride were not permitted there. If he found that those who were backward in piety could not be won by gentle words, he used rigours to root out the evil sloth, and so provoked, either by his humble example, or his command, he led almost the whole of the Brethren to great heights of perfection in unwearying zeal.

There was one man, however, whom he could not win, either by entreaty or by severity; who, despising the Rule and Constitutions of the Fathers, lay in the infirmary, on pretence of sickness, abhorred all piety, not being willing to sing the praises of God with his Brethren, but full of the spirit of the world. This man was named Hugh. When the Blessed Gerard, Abbot of Clairvaulx, came to make the regular visitation at Igni, he put him to penance as a transgressor, which so enraged this son of Belial, that, lying in ambush with a knife, he struck the Blessed Gerard as he entered the Dormitory after Vigils, and wounded him so that he died on the following day.

Great was the grief of Peter, but, Gerard appearing to him in great glory, bade him weep no more for it was well with him. The body of the Blessed martyr was carried to Clairvaulx with great pomp, some, indeed, lamenting his death, but others rejoicing in his victory, because for the sake of discipline he had laid down his life. Peter sung the Mass at his funeral when they reached Clairvaulx, at which, when he had come to the Canon, the holy Father Bernard and the Blessed Malachy appeared to him, on each side of the altar, assuring him that Gerard was now amongst the blessed.

In the room of the Blessed Gerard, a Monk named Henry was chosen Abbot of Clairvaulx. This Henry was soon after created a Cardinal of the Holy Roman Church. The good odour of Peter's name being already much spread abroad, he was elected to fill his place. He walked in the footsteps of the Fathers who had gone before him, especially setting before his eyes the example of the most glorious Bernard. The perfection of his virtues was such that it overflowed, and was made to appear in all he did. His walk, his dress, his very manner of speech, were redolent of that holy humility which had taken such deep root in his heart. Almost all temporal affairs were placed by him in the care of the Stewards of the Monastery. For himself, whenever his time was free, he sat in the parlour, that the younger and weaker Brethren might have free access to him when in trouble, or tossed by temptations. With sweet eloquence he confirmed and strengthened them for the combat. His rigour towards himself may be seen from this, that he never wore two robes and two Cowles all at once, but in the most severe

8

seasons was content with one Cowle and two robes, or two Cowles and one robe. He ate but very sparingly, even of the common food, taking care of the sustenance of his body rather than of the desires of the appetite.

The holy man had a very mean opinion of himself, which at times he used to express. Talking one day with the King of the French, who was his kinsman, he said, "You see, Sire, what a man I am, of so little account, and of such small ability, and yet I have undertaken to govern this great house. I sadly fear that through my insufficiency or imprudence I may bring ruin on this House of Clairvaulx, whose state has been hitherto so fair." The King, much pleased with the humility he showed, answered, "Why be faint-hearted, Reverend Father, and wish to abandon the souls given by God to your guidance? Do you only be Abbot within, in what pertains to their salvation, and I will be Abbot without, in protecting their temporal welfare by my royal authority." Comforted by these words, the Abbot laid aside the idea he had formed of resigning his charge.

His simplicity and love of peace was great. Once a certain knight had a strife with him concerning certain goods, and, on a day agreed on, they were to meet, and settle the dispute, or bring it before the judge. On the day appointed, the knight came with his friends, and the Abbot came walking with a simple Brother. The venerable Abbot said then, before them all, to the knight,

"You are a Christian man. If then these goods, about which there has been a contention, are yours, your word is enough, take them." He, caring more for the goods than for the word of truth, said, "I tell you that, of a truth, they are mine." The Abbot then said, "As they are yours, keep them. I will not seek to have them any more," and so he returned to Clairvaulx. The knight then went back to his wife in triumph, relating to her the simple pure words of the Abbot, and his own answer. She, however, said, "You have acted deceitfully with the holy Abbot, and the vengeance of God will overtake us, if we keep those goods. Unless you restore them, I will not live with you." The man, now quite in fear, went to Clairvaulx, and renounced all right to his ill-gotten treasures.

One day it happened, that a day labourer, not being able to get his hire from the Steward, nor to get an interview with the Blessed Peter, who was sick, was so enraged that he went to a Grange of the Abbey with the intent to set it on fire. As he was about to do this, Peter presented himself before him, and asked him what he was about to do. The man, in astonishment, and thinking his design was known, confessed the whole matter. The holy man then said to him, "Beware of committing so great a sin. Come to me to-morrow to the Infirmary, and I will see that you are paid." The next day came the man to the holy Abbot to ask him to fulfil his promise. The Abbot, not knowing what he meant, drew from him an account of the whole affair. He then dismissed him with an assurance of being paid, and let fall this remark to the Brother that waited on him, "Indeed, Brother, if we only take care of God's will, He will take care of us." The Brother, thinking the labourer must have discovered something important, went after him, and obtained from him a history of all. He doubted not but that it was an Angel of the Lord, who had appeared to him under the form of the Abbot, and so kept him from sin, and procured his payment.

Before Peter was made Abbot of Igni, when he was on the road to vote at the election, he said to the Father who bore him company, and who was a Monk of Igni, "I should like to know who to vote for at this election. Tell me, Father, which of the Monks you think most worthy to be chosen Abbot." The Father replied at once, "I know no one more worthy than yourself." The man of God answered, "I am well assured that you would wish me to be chosen, but as that does not depend on you, I wish really that you would name to me another."—"I know no other," answered the Monk, nor would he mention any other; and when the election took place, with one voice Peter was chosen by the Brethren.

It happened on a time that some of our Abbots, of whom the Venerable Peter was one of the chief, were sent on affairs of the Order to the Emperor Henry. The Abbot of Citeaux not being

himself able to go with them, sent his Prior.
When they were come to Spires, they entered into
the church. After a short prayer the Abbots rose
to examine and admire the magnificence of the
building. Peter, whose delight was not in corruptible things, but whose thoughts were on the
heavenly Jerusalem, kept himself still in prayer.
When at length they were all leaving the church,
they were met by some of the Canons, and were
with great instancy invited to come and dine with
them. One of the Abbots at dinner asked in
whose honour the Church was dedicated. Some
of the clergy answered, "In honour of the most
Holy Mary;" upon which the Abbot of Clairvaulx
inconsiderately subjoined, "I knew it." The
Prior of Citeaux, considering the word, was silent
at the time, but when they had gone out of the
city, he said to the venerable Peter, "My Lord
Abbot, tell me how you knew that the Minster of
Spires was consecrated in honour of Our Lady?"
The man of God, grieving for the word that he
had said, answered, "It seemed to me fitting that
the Mother of God should be Patroness of so
magnificent a building." The Prior, however,
suspecting some other thing lay hid, bound the
venerable man under obedience, as at that time
bearing the authority of the Abbot of Citeaux, to
tell him all without dissimulation. Then, straitened
by obedience, he replied, "When prostrate before
the altar, I bewailed the negligences of the way,
the Blessed Virgin herself, appearing unto me, gave

to me that benediction which is used in our Order, for those returning from a journey.

" ' Almighty Everlasting God, have mercy upon this Thy servant, and whatsoever of ill may have befallen him on the way, whether in sight, hearing, or in the speaking of idle words, do Thou, of Thy unspeakable goodness, graciously pardon. Through Jesus Christ Our Lord.' "

His days were now come to their end, so that, having sowed in tears, he might reap in joy. He passed away from this earth March 18, A.D. 1186, and was buried in the same tomb with S. Gerard the Martyr.

LIFE OF THE BLESSED ABONDE,

MONK OF VILLERS.

THE Blessed Abonde was born in the year of grace, 1189, in the town of Huy, in the diocese of Liege, of parents in the middle class of life. His father was a man who loved the world, and strove to inspire his children with his own sentiments. His mother, named Mary, was of an opposite character, caring only for the things of God. Abonde followed the teaching of his mother. From his tender childhood he appeared naturally formed for good, with a character simple, modest, staid, and sweet, which caused him to be much beloved by all.

At twelve years of age the young boy was observed not to care about play with his school companions, but all his time of leisure he spent in the church, praying in a simple manner to Jesus Christ on the cross, and having a most tender devotion to the Holy Virgin.

His father had him taught such things as might be useful to him in worldly business. The young man, however, not desiring at all the things of this world, but seeking to save his soul, determined to take refuge in some Monastery. That he might choose with more prudence, he had

recourse to the counsel of a Nun named Juette,
who was often favoured by God with revelations.
She quite approved of his design, suggesting the
Monasteries of Orval or the Three Fountains.
The young man, however, leaned to the Monastery of Villers ; and, seeing him set to this, she
bade him go there with the blessing of God. As
he was thinking of executing his design, he made
a journey to Liege, where he met with Conrad,
Prior of Villers. The Prior confirmed him in his
resolve, and, having come to Villers, he was received to the habit in A.D. 1210. His mother,
brothers, and sisters, learning this, themselves
followed his example, and all of them entered the
Order of Citeaux.

A great number of miraculous things are related
of him, and he was favoured with many appari-
tions of the most Holy Virgin. A Monk, named
Bernard, lately dead, appeared to him, and told
him that, for recompense of the many sufferings
he had endured in the Order, the Lord had given
him a crown amongst the Martyrs.

The prayers of the Blessed Abonde were so ef-
fectual, that he obtained the conversion of many
sinners, and cures for the sick. Before he died
he suffered a most cruel malady, and was so weak
that he could not lift his hand to his mouth.
God comforted him in his sickness by the appearance of our Saviour on the cross. This caused
him to endure his afflictions in patience. The
Brother, who attended on him, was weary of his

task, and thought to quit it, in order to follow the regular exercises of the Community, imagining that he was losing his time. But our Lord revealed to him that one day in the service of the sick was worth forty days of the common exercises of the Community. This encouraged him to wait on the Blessed Abonde to the last.

He died on the nineteenth of March, A.D. 1239, being about fifty years of age.

OF THE BLESSED RAYNALD AND OF
CERTAIN OTHER BRETHREN.

THE Blessed Raynald, even when yet in the world, was not of the world, but was wholly given to God, especially taking care to preserve the purity of his body from all stain. So great was his chastity, that it is said he was never afflicted with any irregular desires from his very youth. At the age of thirty he entered the Abbey of S. Amand, of the Congregation of Cluni. He lived there for twenty years in unblamable righteousness of life. In A.D. 1147 he passed thence to Clairvaulx, and underwent no small troubles on that account from his former Brethren, who took it ill that he should have forsaken their company. In no wise moved by their efforts to draw him back to them, he began, in the new observance, to lead a more perfect life than before, counting all his past time as unprofitably spent. He watched, and fasted, and laboured, with the greatest diligence, giving to God every day the reasonable sacrifice of his soul and body, praying continually in the spirit, with sighs and tears.

One day, when he was out reaping with the Brethren, he had a vision, in which he saw the great Queen of Heaven, with S. Elizabeth, and Mary Magdalen, descend into the field, and go

round to each of the Brethren, who were toiling
under the heat of the sun, as if to console them.
This vision filled him with joy, and he understood
in a measure how so many learned persons, and
those delicately brought up in the world, were enabled to endure the hardships of the Cistercian Observance. He told no one, however, of what he had
seen, till his last sickness came. Some weeks
before his death, the most holy Virgin Mary,
Mother of God, appeared to him clad in most
beautiful apparel. The Blessed man, in great admiration, cried to her, "When shall I be allowed
to put on such beautiful garments?" She answered, "You shall do so when you come to me."
Six days before his death, whilst at Compline, he
twice heard the striking of the death tablet. Supposing some of those who were ill was dying, he
hastened to the Infirmary, but, finding no one to
be dying, he believed that it was a warning of his
own approaching end. On that night he became
ill with a fever, which in a few days carried him
away. During his sickness he had always in his
mouth the angelical salutation, and it was whilst
pronouncing this holy prayer that he breathed
forth his soul into the arms of Jesus Christ, presented to Him as it were by the hands of His holy
Mother.

On the same day that he died, there died also
a Convert-Brother, who had faithfully served the
Lord, so that the prayers for the dead were said
for both of these Monks at the same time, and

they were also buried together in the same grave. It would seem that the two strokes of the death tablet, which the Blessed Raynald heard, were the warning of God for himself and this Brother, who were made worthy at the same time to enter that rest which is prepared for the people of God.

Another Monk, named Gerard, who was Sacristan, a few days after when at Compline heard the death tablet. Being certain that no one was dying, and having heard that the Blessed Raynald had thus received a signal to prepare for death, he felt sure it was for him. He was taken with a fever which in ten days carried him away. For the last three or four hours of his agony, he held his joined hands stretched towards a Crucifix, which was before him, never stirring the least, though the rest of his body was agitated and trembling.

Another Brother followed a few days afterwards, named Everhard, who being very fearful concerning the sins of his past life, was ravished in the spirit, and was brought into the presence of our Lord Jesus Christ, who consoled him, saying to him in a clear voice, "Thy sins are forgiven." When he came to himself he found his soul full of sweetest consolation. All these holy Brethren died in the year of our Redemption, 1162.

LIFE OF THE BLESSED GOZEVIN,

ABBOT OF CITEAUX.

THE Blessed Gozevin, being a Monk of Citeaux, was sent to take the charge of the Abbey of Bonnevaux, in place of the Abbot John, when that holy man had been made Bishop of Valence, A.D. 1138. His reputation was such that, at the death of Rainard in A.D. 1150, he was translated to Citeaux.

The next year, considering that there were now five hundred Monasteries of the Order, and believing these to be quite enough for the number of true vocations, he obtained an order to be made in the General Chapter that no new Monasteries should be founded. This he did, from a fear lest the Cistercian discipline should become relaxed. The order had however little practical effect.

It was in the year of Redemption, 1153, that the most venerable Father Bernard was taken away from amongst men. The Blessed Gozevin assisted him to the end of his life, and after his departure caused him to be clothed in the robe of the great Archbishop Malachy, over which were placed his priestly vestments, his hands and face remaining uncovered. Great were the crowds of people, who, assembling from all sides, poured

into the valley of Clairvaulx. As the tidings of
the death of the man of God became wider spread,
the multitude increased especially on account of
the miracles wrought by him after his death.
Gozevin, fearing lest the Monastic discipline
might suffer from the ingress of such multitudes
of people, caused the body to be buried early on
the morning of the third day, and approaching the
tomb gave orders to the dead Saint to work no
more miracles publicly, which command he faithfully obeyed.

The Blessed Gozevin did not survive the Venerable Father very long, but went to his rest on
March the thirty-first, A.D. 1155.

LIFE OF SAINT HUGH,

ABBOT OF BONNEVAUX.

AMONGST others eminent for their character and their learning, who in the golden age of the Cistercian Order, were drawn by the sweet odour of the most holy Father Bernard from the pleasures of the world, the venerable Hugh was not the least. He shone like a star in the Religious firmament, having taken the habit in the sacred Cloister of Clairvaulx. Here provoked by the examples of his fellow soldiers in the great warfare, and instructed by the holy teaching of his master, he ran eagerly the way of the commandments of God. He drew the hearts of all the Monks upon him, who admired in one so young such constancy of mind, and purity of life.

The old Enemy of souls was afflicted at the loss of one he prized, and left nothing untried to draw Christ's champion from his purpose. At one time it was the hardness of this way of life, at another the continual silence, or the constant mortifications of the Order, against which the foul fiend placed in attractive colours the delights and comforts of a worldly life. These darts came one after another in thick succession upon the inexperienced soldier, and he began to think of giving up his

Angelical way of life, to return to the vomit of
an earthly conversation. Whilst thus driven and
tossed by the storm and tempest, the Wicked One
hurled yet more fiercely his fiery darts. Oppressed
with the weight of his temptations, he was on the
point of yielding a reluctant consent, and of bidding farewell to the Monastic life. But the merciful and gracious God took pity on him. One
day as he entered the Church, and prayed before
the altar with many tears, he saw over the altar in
a vision the Mother of mercy, clad in a garment
bright as the light. On her right hand was her
Son Jesus. Then there was unfolded before his
view the mystery of the Annunciation by the
Angel, the birth of Jesus of the Virgin, the giving
of the glad tidings to the Shepherds, and His holy
Circumcision. After this he beheld also how the
Lord was apprehended by the Jews, scourged,
mocked and crucified, and how afterwards He rose
again, and ascended into heaven. As he gazed on
these things, our Lady said to him, Be strong,
and let thy heart be comforted in the Lord, for
from henceforth thou shalt not be beaten by temptations.

Fortified by this marvellous and delightful
vision the young soldier of Christ now took to
him all the armour of God, with which he over-
came the deceits of the Enemy. He kept the
mysteries of his redemption ever before his eyes,
continually pondering over them in his heart.
And considering what and what kind of sufferings

the Son of God had endured for the salvation of
the human race, he clung closer to Him by a more
vehement love, becoming dead to the world, that
he might live only to Him. All the delights of
the world were esteemed by him as nothing. He
rested only in the arms of his Beloved, drinking
deep draughts of the wholesome waters of wisdom,
and piercing into the hidden things of the divine
secrets. For as often as he began to think on the
Passion of the Lord, straightway he seemed ravished out of himself, and changed into another
man.

After these things therefore he was no more
shaken in his holy purpose, but began to afflict
himself with exceeding great abstinences, inso-
much that sometimes he seemed to lose all memory
and understanding. The holy Father Bernard,
who was still at that time amongst men, came to
him by the providence of God, and bade him to be
sent into the Infirmary, ordering that every night
the Vigils should be recited to him, before the
others who were sick, that he might afterwards
sleep sufficiently. He also gave him a general
leave to speak, and so by the mercy of God he in
a short while grew better.

Bernard was attached to the Blessed Hugh
with a singular love, and these two would sometimes spend whole days in talking on divine
things. Especially the holy Father admired in
his disciple that clear wisdom, which in earthly as

9

well as in divine matters resolved all difficulties with marvellous subtlety.

When therefore a new foundation was to be made at Bonnevaux, the Blessed Hugh was chosen, and set over the others by his master, that he might be their leader. This honour however he by no means consented to receive, desiring to lay his bones amongst those of the holy company at Clairvaulx. It was only under the compulsion of obedience that he undertook it.

When made Abbot he lived in greater hardness than heretofore. Some therefore chid him as being too austere, but he replied, "Hitherto I was subject to the care of another, and so I walked with boldness and simplicity. Now I am set over others, I am bound to correct not only my own defects but those of others also, and shall have to give an account to a strict Judge of all the sheaves committed to me. There is need then of greater watchfulness, and of more frequent mortifications, that I may not sleep in death, or neglecting the salvation of others, miserably lose myself."

To the Monastery of Bonnevaux came a youth of noble birth, named Hilary, who in his first fervour lived a most holy life. But by-and-bye the malignant fiend excited in him the desires of the pleasures of the world which he had left. The young man however made known all his evil thoughts to the Abbot. This holy man, not ignorant of the devices of the Enemy, exhorted him with kindest words not to give any consent, but his words availing little, he thus spoke: "My son, have mercy on thy own soul, pleasing God. Do not lose the glory prepared for thee. I promise thee, if thou wilt only stay, thou shalt be a companion of the holy Angels."

The Novice was comforted by these words, passed well the year of trial, and made his vows with ready mind. He shortly after this fell sick, and for two years endured the most grievous pains, kissing with humility and patience the scourge of the Lord like a faithful son. As the time of his departure drew nigh, the holy Job was sent with great glory to console him. The whole of the Dormitory was filled with a divine light, and the Blessed Job addressing him, said, "I am sent by the Father of mercies and God of all consolation to comfort thee. Thou hast been patient as I was. Thou shalt reap what thou hast sowed, and tomorrow shalt be with me in glory." After this the Monk died in great joy, having been fortified by the Sacraments of the Church. He appeared not long after to the Abbot Hugh in the splendour of divine glory, and told him with great thanks of the crown which he had obtained through his wise counsels.

Two others who had joined the Cloister of Bon-nevaux were tormented by a like temptation to return to the world. One was a soldier, called Paul, the other a priest. The soldier had a dream in which it appeared to him that he was flung headlong into a pit of horrible depth, so that it was three days before he reached the bottom. He told the dream to the Abbot. The Abbot told him it was a prophecy of what would happen by rejecting his counsel. " The vision," he said, " declares the calamity of thy everlasting damnation. If, treading in the steps of the demon, thou leave the most safe harbour of the Cistercian Order, after three days thou wilt perish, and be cast into the pit of hell. If thou wilt stay, I promise thee on the part of God a share in eternal glory." The man, like another Cain, fleeing from the face of the Lord, returned to the world, and was killed in fighting with an enemy of his, dying excommunicated, three days after.

The Priest however was not disobedient to the counsels of his Abbot, and obtained a most happy end. For, after some years, when he came to his last agony, holy Mary appeared to him, saying, " Behold I come to fulfil that which the Abbot Hugh promised to thee. Be of good courage, therefore ; tomorrow thou shalt enjoy everlasting peace amongst the companies of the heavenly citizens." On the following day, with great gladness, he rendered up his spirit to God.

When the Abbot was once assisting at the Solemn Vigils on the Feast of the Annunciation, he went round the Choir, as was his wont, to stir up the Brethren more fervently to the praises of God. As he came into the midst of the Choir, he beheld standing there a demon of horrible aspect, at whose presence being terrified he fell almost lifeless on the ground. The Brethren raised him up, and being strengthened he returned to his seat. But the following day he made known to them the vision in the Chapter, telling them that he felt sure that some one of them was in mortal sin, or such a visitant would never have been present there. He begged therefore that Brother to wipe away the guilt by true contrition joined to a humble confession. Hearing this all but the guilty one made confession. Again the next night the demon was present in the Choir. Then the Abbot seeking for the guilty Monk made known to him the sin of his soul, which had been revealed to him by God. The Monk seeing he was not hid confessed his guilt, asking pardon and penance with great contrition, and after that the devil appeared no more.

The holy Abbot was endowed with the foresight of future things, and two of his Monks, who seemed in no danger of present death, though somewhat sick, he warned of their approaching end, telling them both the day and hour, that they might be the better prepared, receiving on that account the holy sacraments of the Church.

There was at Bonnevaux a Brother, who had committed some fault in his own Monastery, and had been transferred to that of Bonnevaux by his Superiors. This Brother falling sick, the Abbot entreated to confess the sin by which he had given scandal. The Brother denied that he was in any way guilty, and that his conscience was clean from all sin. He desired moreover instantly that he might receive the Body of the Lord. As he was obstinate the Abbot yielded to his request. But when the priest had brought the most venerable Sacrament, and had placed the consecrat'd Host in the mouth of the sick man, he began straightway to cry out: "Ah, wretched man, what shall I do? what shall I do?" Upon which words the priest took from his mouth the Body of the Lord, which he had not consumed, and immediately he expired.

It happened once when the Abbot was on a journey that a certain servant of the Monastery fell sick, and died, having confessed his sins to one of the Priests of the Abbey. But when the Abbot was returned, as he sat on his bed the first night after Compline, he beheld this young man ascend the steps of the Dormitory. He came to him and fell at his feet confessing his sins with such abundance of tears that the Abbot was moved to tears also. After absolution the dead man asked the Abbot to pray for him for he was in great torment. The Abbot stretched out his hand to make certain if he were in the body or a spirit, when the dead man at once vanished.

In the same Monastery there died also another young man, who on the very day of his departure appeared to the Abbot as he was resting in bed at the meridian hour. He fell on his knees before the Abbot, complaining that he had been delivered by God to the tormentors, and was suffering principally because the priest who had heard his last confession had not set him a worthy penance. He then made his confession to the Abbot. The Abbot asked him if he would find mercy; he answered, he should if the Abbot and the Brethren would watch in prayer for him, and saying this, he vanished. The Reverend Abbot knew not whether he were asleep or awake when this took place, but opening his eyes, found the place where the dead man had wept in confession covered with tears, and even his Cowl wet with tears. He therefore offered many Masses for him and obtained for him the united prayers of the Brethren. We must not suppose, however, that the Confession made by the dead man was of sacramental virtue, but that the Abbot, seeing the depth of his misery, might be the more induced to offer pacific victims to God on his behalf.

The Festival of the receiving of the Crown of Thorns already kept in all the dioceses of France was by the zeal of the venerable Abbot introduced into the Breviary of the Cistercian Order. This was done by the Fathers at a meeting of the General Chapter. S. Hugh, on his return to his Abbey, received a message from God to the intent that his time of departure was at hand. As far as possible, from this time forth, he separated himself from all worldly business. If any one applied to him on matters of this perishable world, he sent him to the Prior, being desirous to give himself wholly to the study of the things of hea-

ven. When death was coming upon him he was
carried into the Church, and there received the
most venerable Sacraments of the Lord, after
which he blessed his sons, and bade them all farewell. Then signing himself with the holy sign
he slept in peace, and they knew not that he was
indeed dead, so quietly had he passed away to his
rest. Of the exact date of his death history is
silent, but it was about the year A.D. 1180. His
feast was kept on the twenty-eighth or twenty-
ninth of April. The Catalogue of the Order men-
tions his name among the Canonized Saints.
Many miracles were wrought at his sepulchre at
Bonnevaux. But in A.D. 1576 the heretics entering the Monastery dispersed and destroyed his
holy relics.

LIFE OF

BLESSED ARNULPH OF LOUVAIN,

ABBOT OF VILLERS.

B LESSED Arnulph of noble birth never even in his early years gave his mind to pleasures of the world. As soon as he came to man's estate he desired to find a refuge from cares and troubles in the Cloisters of the Cistercian Order. William, Abbot of Villers, having affairs with the Duke, whilst he was celebrating the holy Mass with great devotion, the most blessed Mother of God appeared to him with these words: "There will come to thee men asking thee to receive a certain boy, receive him without delay, for he is a chosen vessel to me." Mass being over, as the Abbot was about to depart, the citizens bring a young man named Arnulph, of excellent manners and of comely appearance, beseeching the Abbot to take him. The Abbot did so, adopting him for a son as commended to him by the Mother of the Lord. Whilst a Novice he often used to repeat the words used by S. Bernard : " Bernard, Bernard, wherefore camest thou hither?" He afterwards became Sub-prior of the Monastery of Villers.

When the venerable Nicholas, Abbot of Villers,

had gone the way of all flesh, whilst the Monks waited for the coming of the Abbot of Clairvaulx to preside at the election of another Abbot, there came a Feast of Blessed Mary, ever a Virgin. And whilst the Brethren sang the Vesper Office with great spiritual gladness, the Spirit of God came upon a Brother named James, and by the light of the Holy Ghost he foretold that Arnulph would be made Abbot. This accordingly took place A.D. 1240, upon which this Brother was ever afterwards called James the prophet.

This new Abbot, a truly simple man, just, and departing from evil, placed all his confidence in God and the ever-blessed Virgin, distrusting his own insufficiency. When once entering the Chapter, he heard those words of the Rule, "Let the Abbot know that the blame will be laid on the Pastor if the householder find any want of profit in the flock;" and again, that word, "Let him know, that of all his judgments, he shall render an account to God, the most just Judge," his heart quaked for fear. His whole look and walk was one of humility and gentle meekness, yet when necessity urged, he used the knife to cut out by the root the sins of transgressors. But the management of the temporal concerns of his Abbey he committed wholly to the Stewards and Convert Brothers, giving himself to God alone, and studying the salvation of souls.

This holy man therefore used to sit alone in the parlour, in silence, with his eyes cast on the ground, so that if any of the younger Brethren or those that were weak were beaten about by a multitude of temptations, or weighed down by some trouble, they might have free access to him. Then, according to the knowledge and grace given to him with wholesome warning and sweet words of edification, he strengthened them to endure the wrestling they had undertaken for Christ. For this mild Pastor did not by an unbending spirit disturb the Community entrusted to him, nor did he make any unjust arrangement, as if making use of an absolute power, but he did all things in observance of the Rule and with counsel; always keeping in remembrance that saying of the most holy Father Bernard, "One who is elected Abbot is not placed over the constitutions of the Fathers, but over the transgressions of the Brethren." And this other saying, "For neither is the Abbot above the Rule, for to this Rule he has also bound himself by voluntary profession."

Reading over and over S. Bernard's treatise concerning vows and dispensations, he, according to the form there laid down, dispensed with his subjects. He was therefore greatly beloved by his Monks and by secular people, and princes paid him reverence.

Henry Duke of Brabant, when he called together for counsel the nobles of the land, called also the man of God. The nobles seeing him come said, that the issue of the council depended on him. The Abbot, after having been received with great honour, inquired of the Duke, why in such grave matters of business he had sent for him, a man so simple, and unskilled in such matters. The Duke answered, " I have sent for you, my beloved Father, and received you with such honour, that my nobles and judges may see with what love I cherish you and your Community ; so that far from doing you any injury, they may contrariwise protect and defend you. Do you only be Abbot within, in those things which pertain to God and the salvation of souls, and I will be Abbot without, by defending your possessions, and by inflicting vengeance on any one who may presume to trouble you."

He perfectly carried out his words. When once a Brother passing by a tavern refused money to those drinking there, and one of the most powerful of them leaping out took away from him his horse and kept it; the Duke hearing of it caused the man to be hung. The nobles who did any injury to the Brethren, he forced to enter their Chapter and make satisfaction.

The Duke used every year to get a robe made of the Monk's cloth, in which he went to the tournaments, saying that clad in this nothing could hurt him.

Having no male heir, he vowed if God would give him a man child, he would build a Monastery. His vow was accepted, and having received a son, he built the Abbey called Duke's Valley. When his end drew nigh he was asked where he would wish to be buried; he answered, "at Villers, a Monastery I have above all loved and honoured, I wish to be buried, and I commend myself to the prayers of the most dear Abbot Arnulph, and to those of the Community." Thus after receiving the most holy sacraments he expired. The funeral service being over at Louvain, the body was carried to Villers, and was met by the Community in solemn procession. When he was laid in the grave the Monks all burst into tears, seeing their patron and protector taken 'away. Many indeed were the psalters and other pious prayers which they offered for his repose.

The Blessed Arnulph, after having been Abbot ten years, resigned the pastoral staff, much against the will of his Community, and of the neighbouring Abbots. He loved the quiet of contemplation with beautiful Rachel, rather than the blear-eyed Lia in the tumult of worldly business.

With serene face and tranquil mind he then went to say Mass, and as it were awaking out of a deep sleep, he began thenceforward to reach after new perfections, as if the time past of his life had been nothing. All the remainder of his life was spent in praying, meditating, writing or hearing confessions. So persevering in every good work, he slept in the Lord, and was buried near the window of the Chapter on the outside.

LIFE OF SAINT MARTIN,

BISHOP OF SAGUNT IN SPAIN, CANONIZED AS
S. SACERDOS.

SAINT MARTIN was born of noble and most virtuous parents, his father's name being Michael, and that of his mother, Sanctia. The boy gave tokens of his future sanctity at a very early age. His parents, by their wealth and their noble blood, were persons of great authority at the court of Alphonse, king of Spain. Giving themselves to alms, vigils, and prayer, they were blessed by God with good children. Two sons were born to them, Nunnius Sanctius and Martin of Finnoxe, and two daughters, Teresa and Eve, who all with their mother's milk were filled with the spirit of godliness, rendering themselves well worthy of their forefathers. Nunnius Sanctius, the first-born, was brought up in the king's court, treading in the steps of his father, as a man of war from his youth; but Martin was educated in the study of learning, excelling those of his own age in science and letters, that afterwards he might, like a tree planted in the house of the Lord, bring forth his fruit in due season. As the young man increased daily in wisdom and grace, so as to exceed the expectation of all men, his father fell ill

of a grievous disease, and died. Martin returned
home to comfort his mother in the affliction she
had sustained. His father's body was laid in the
ancient sepulchre of his family, in the Monastery
of S. Dominic of Silos, of the Benedictine Order.

The young man, pondering in his mind the un-
certainty of all happiness in this earthly scene,
took a good thought into his breast, to consecrate
himself wholly unto the Lord. He brought the
vows of his heart to pass by entering the Abbey of
Cantavos, founded on the confines of old Castile,
in the year of Redemption 1151, by King Alphonse.
He did not do this without first letting his mother
know the secrets of his heart, lest she might be
angry with his design. His good mother approved of all, and would herself make the offering
of her son at the altar of God. On a certain day
therefore she took her journey with her two sons,
Nunnius and Martin, to the country of Arragon,
to the Monastery of Cantavos. Then Venerable
Blaise, Abbot of that Cloister, with his Community, received the young man at her hands.
Sanctia herself bound his hand in the cloth of
the Altar, according to the rite commanded by the
most Blessed Benedict in his Rule, and thus made
an offering of her son to the most high God. Together with the offering of her son she made a
gift of certain lands in the following manner.
" Moreover I present to God and Blessed Mary of
Cantavos, and to the Lord Blaise, Abbot of the
said place, and his successors, and to the Commu-

nity, following the Cistercian Rule, the farm called Bonnizes, with all its lands, pastures, and appurtenances, to have and to hold for ever, and to do with as they shall please; to sell, to exchange, or to give : and this I do for the forgiveness of my own sins, and those of my parents. If any one dare to change, or infringe this my deed, may he be excommunicated by God, and brought under a curse, with Dathan and Abiron, whom the earth swallowed up alive, and may he with the traitor Judas be given over to never-ending pains in hell."

This deed was confirmed and signed by herself, by her first-born Nunnius, and by Martin also.

It was in A.D. 1158 that Martin gave himself to the Lord, and entered the Monastery of Cantavos, and after the year of his Noviciate was completed, he made his vows, being then one-and-twenty years old. Shortly after this, the Abbot Blaise, seeing that his Monastery was much distressed by the want of necessary water, determined to pass into another place, which he accordingly did with the consent of Sanctius, king of Castile, Pope Alexander III. confirming the thing by a Bull from Rome in A.D. 1164. The place of the new Monastery was called Horte, and there, after awhile, the Venerable old Abbot passed away to a better world. At his death the Brethren with one consent called upon Martin to take the place of their departed Father. He, yet a young man, for he had not yet been six years in the Religious

life, and having the opinion that he was a great
sinner, dull of understanding, and heavy in heart,
refused to accede to their choice. At length their
entreaties and commands with difficulty prevailed
over him, and he yielded himself to their will, for
he could not withstand the sight of their tears.
The servant of Christ was not lifted up with pride
at the exaltation of his dignity, but showed himself humble and meek to all. He was a father
rather than a master, and yet, with all his kindness, he never let go the discipline of the Rule,
which he had bound himself to enforce.

His holy report brought likewise many of those,
who desired to live a more perfect life in the world,
to seek at his hands a rule of life, by which they
might serve God acceptably. He received them
all with his wonted gentle spirit, and taught them
the way of salvation.

The princes and great men of the earth vied
with each other in rendering honour to the holy
man, taking refuge in his prayers, as a strong wall
of defence against all the wiles of the enemy.
Many enriched the Monastery with great possessions. Alphonse also, king of Castile, came with
his queen Eleanor to visit the Monastery, ordering
spacious buildings to be set up at his own expense
as a dwelling-place for the Monks. Indeed, both
he and Peter his successor became Oblates of the
Cistercian Order. Order also was made that no
tax or toll should be levied on the goods of the
Monastery. The Spanish Bishops also with one

10

heart venerated the man of God. Roderic, afterwards Archbishop of Toledo, came and resided at
Horte, until the Church and buildings of the
Abbey should be completed under his superintend-
ance. The Bishops also, in whose dioceses the
possessions of the Monastery were situate, freed
the Monks from the obligation of tithes.

The See of Sagunt falling vacant A.D. 1185, the
people demanded for their pastor the holy Abbot
of Horte. King Alphonse was equally desirous to
have so good a man made Bishop. With humble
mind, however, the Blessed Martin refused the
proffered dignity, having his mind set upon the
contemplation of heavenly things. At length an
order being obtained from the sovereign Pontiff,
he was constrained to surrender, and a Monk
named Ximenes was chosen Abbot in his place.

The Blessed Martin had been twenty years ruling his Abbey, when he was made Bishop. In
the government of his diocese, he showed the
same discipline mingled with gentleness, which
had given such lustre to his Abbey. He soon
took away such abuses as he found existing in it.
Among other things, he restored to his Cathedral
Church Regular Canons, who had been in part
superseded by secular clergy.

The life of a Bishop, however, was not suited
to his retiring spirit, and after seven years he
resigned his see with the consent of the king, and
the permission of the sovereign Pontiff. Having
returned to the Monastery of Horte, he gave him-

self up to a life of prayer and great austerity,
afflicting his body by fasting, and clad in coarse
clothing. Sometimes, whilst at prayer, he would
be so affected with his contemplation as to be rapt
out of himself in an ecstasy of mind. In the
seventy-third year of his age he went to visit the
Abbey of Blessed Mary of Ovila, founded by the
pious king Alphonse. There it was made known
to him by divine revelation that he should shortly
put off this tabernacle. Desiring to breathe forth
his soul amongst his own Brethren at Horte, he
started on his journey thither at once, leaving the
Monks of Ovila very sorrowful for his hasty departure ; for indeed they had gathered from him that
his end was at hand, and had hoped to retain his
precious relics amongst them.

Some of the Monks accompanied him back on
his journey. But when they had gone with him
as far as the city of Sotoca, he was seized with a
most grievous sickness, and being fortified with
the sacraments of the Church, he desired but this
one thing, that his body might be borne for its
last burial to the Monastery of Horte. So whilst
speaking of divine things his beautiful soul passed
away to the realms of the heavenly country A.D.
1210.

Then the Maker of all things, that He might
discover to men the great merits of His servant,
and how precious in the sight of the Lord is the
death of His Saints, filled the whole house where
the body rested with the most sweet odour, which

delicious perfume indeed remained in the house many days after the holy body had been taken away.

The very same hour in which the Blessed Father passed, the Monks of Horte by a revelation from heaven knew of his departure. They received his relics with great veneration accompanied as they were by a vast concourse of people, and buried them with much honour, many miracles being wrought by the Lord's power at his tomb, both at the time when his body was first buried and afterwards.

Now it came to pass after some days that the Lord sent an Angel to the Monastery of Horte, who, entering the Church, separated the head from the body of the Blessed Martin, and bearing it away to the city of Sagunt, presented it to the Bishop and Canons, with these words : " This is the head of a holy priest, formerly Bishop of this place." The Bishop and Canons deposited it with great reverence amongst the relics belonging to the Church, and as numerous miracles were worked through its intervention, a feast was cele-brated in honour of the holy priest, the Angel of God not having mentioned the Blessed Martin's name. In process of time the relics of S. Martin were removed from their first resting-place, and then it was discovered that the head of the holy man had been taken out of the tomb. The mitre was found close to the neck, and the body itself was uncorrupted, clad in priestly vestments, and still emitting a sweet odour. Then the former suspicion that the head brought by the Angel was that of the Blessed Martin, became converted into a certainty, but still, as of old, the feast was kept under the name of S. Sacerdos, or the holy Priest.

Louis of Estrada, Abbot of Horte, translated the relics of S. Martin A.D. 1535 to a costly shrine on the left side of the high Altar, the body being still uncorrupted.

LIFE OF BLESSED WILLIAM,

ABBOT OF CLAIRVAULX.

THE venerable man William was born at Brussels. When it pleased God to call him to
the Monastic life, he came to Villers in Brabant,
and there bound himself to the Cistercian family.
As soon as he entered on the ascetical life, his
step went ever onward from virtue to virtue, till
A.D. 1221 he was chosen to be Abbot of Villers.
How kind and good a pastor he was cannot be
sufficiently related. But how strict and austere
with himself even in sickness. Whence, when
sometimes for the repairing of his strength he was
placed amongst the infirm, and would ask some of
the more ancient to dine with him, they unwillingly consented to his invitation on account of the
sobriety and poverty of his fare. To the poor,
however, his hand was ever open and stretched
out. He was saddened when the petition was for
some small thing, being glad to give great gifts.
For he had read in the gospel, " With what measure ye mete it shall be measured to you again."
He never therefore ate his morsel alone, but the
orphan and the widow ate of it. Especially, he
was kind to the Beguines. The sides also of the
poor were warmed with the fleece of his sheep.

The Monastery of Villers flourished greatly under his care, and became mother of two other houses, *Great Meadow* and *S. Bernard's Place;* the first near Namur, the latter in Brabant.

The Abbot having one day gone to Louvain to speak on some affair with the Duke who resided there, whilst he was celebrating Mass the Blessed Virgin Mary appeared to him, saying : "When you have finished the Mass, the citizens of this town will come to you bringing a boy with them, whom they will ask you to take. Do so at once, for he is a chosen vessel to me." When the Mass was over, a young man named Arnulph was brought to him by the citizens with the request that he would take him. He did so accordingly, receiving him as the child of Blessed Mary, entrusted by her to his care. Having entered the cell of the Novices, this youth had often in mouth and heart that saying of S. Bernard, "Bernard, why camest thou hither?" He never had to be twice corrected for the same fault, but quickly amended himself.

The Abbey of Villers had a Grange called Hex, where there lived some Lay-Brothers occupied in labours of the hands. They had in their possession a beautiful ox, fat and well-favoured. A certain sick woman, who had seen this ox, took a strong fancy to eat some of its flesh, and though all kinds of meat were set before her, nothing would satisfy, but the strange longing continued. At last the Abbot William was informed of the

woman's desire, and that her life indeed was in
peril through this unsatisfied longing. " Well,"
said he, " it is better for the ox to die than the
woman. See that it be done secretly, that the
woman's longing may be satisfied." The Brother
accordingly killed the ox, skinned it, and cut it
up, and taking the piece which the woman longed
for, sent it to her, and no sooner had she eaten it
than she got quite well. On the following morning, however, when the oxen were ploughing, lo!
and behold! the ox, which had been killed, was to
be seen ploughing with the rest. The Brother,
amazed, ran to the house, and going to the room
where he had laid out the carcase, found nothing
whatsoever, neither the flesh, nor even the blood,
which had been spilt on the floor. Three Brothers
of the House were witnesses of these things. So
the ox, slain for the sake of charity, was thus by
the divine power brought back to life.

When one day the venerable Father was about
to celebrate Mass, a young Brother of sincere
piety, who was to serve him at the altar, asked
permission to receive the sacred communion of
the Body of the Lord. The man of God, however,
a strenuous upholder of the rules of the Fathers,
answered him, gently, " My son, thou didst communicate on the Lord's day, according to the custom of the Order. It is not, therefore, necessary
now to satisfy thy devotion, wherein the institu-
tions of the Order seem to be opposed. Nay, I
think thou hadst better rather abstain than trans-

gress the statutes of the Fathers. Believe, and
eat spiritually, though not sacramentally." To
this the good Brother made no answer, but accepted it with all submission, not murmuring nor
impatient. When oh! the goodness of God!
How great is His sweetness, which He has laid
up for them that fear Him! The venerable
Father proceeded to the Altar, and going through
the Mass in order, broke the Sacred Host into
three parts, one of which he placed in the chalice
with the Sacred Blood. But on reaching the time
of Communion, he could find but one fraction remaining, the other having by the divine power
been already given for the Communion of the
devout servant of the Altar. The Father had
refused him, but God Himself would not allow
His servant to be disappointed of his desire, and
had miraculously fed him with the Body of His
Lord.

It chanced on another day, that as the Blessed
William was devoutly intent on the celebration,
there fell a spider from the roof into the holy
chalice, in which was the Sacred Blood. Not
considering the horror of taking this spider in the
draught, the Father, for the reverence of the
Sacred Blood, swallowed the nauseous insect. It
was about a year afterwards that a pustule formed
in one of his fingers, from which, instead of matter, there came forth this spider, whole and entire.

When the venerable Father had for some time
exercised the office of Abbot at Villers, the fame

of his virtues spreading abroad, he, to the great sorrow of his Monks, was made Abbot of Clairvaulx. This post of honour he fitly adorned, loved by the good, and feared by the undisciplined. He had a special gift of tears, and the gift of visions in divine contemplation.

There was at that time celebrated at Rome a General Council, and William received from Pope Gregory IX. an invitation to be present. The Council being over, he was taken captive as he returned through Lombardy, by the Emperor Frederic. Some of the Monks of Villers, hearing that he was in prison, through the influence of Henry Duke of Brabant, obtained his liberty. But before he could return he had departed out of the body. His lifeless remains were brought back to the Abbey of Clairvaulx, where they were honourably buried. After his death the flesh of his body shone with a divine splendour, token of his spotless virginity, and of his most pure mind.

On the night he died, he appeared to a certain cloistered nun, not far from the Monastery of Villers, surrounded with the brightness of a most glorious light, so dazzling that the eye could not steadfastly gaze on its effulgence. His garment appeared to be of the most precious stuff adorned with the richest gems, and on his head he wore a crown of gold most beautiful with many jewels. The holy woman, when she saw him, not yet knowing that he had been loosed from the prison-house of the body, was seized with great wonder and admiration.

"Reverend Father," she said, after awhile, "how is it that I see you so gloriously arrayed? You were not wont so to be." To which the Blessed man answered, "I have left the world, and go to receive a never-fading crown." Scarce able to speak from grief at this tidings, she however added, "What mean the precious stones and the crown which you wear?" The Father replied, "The precious stones are the tribulations and distresses which I suffered innocently through persecutions, for defending the liberty of the Church. The golden crown is the crown of Martyrs, which has been given me as a recompense for the hard labours of the observance of the Order." With these words he disappeared. He left this vale of tears A.D. 1209.

LIFE OF THE BLESSED WILLIAM,

MONK OF GRANDSELVE.

THE Blessed William was Marquis of Mont-
pellier, and by his wife Sybille, daughter of
the King of Jerusalem, he had several children.
So nobly were these children married, that most
of the royal families of Europe trace to them their
genealogy. Despising the advantages of his birth
and rank, the Marquis chose the hidden life of
Cistercian poverty rather than all the glory of the
world.

After being four years at Grandselve, he was
sent with others to found the new Abbey of Valdaune, A.D. 1152. He still, however, used to
return sometimes to Grandselve. Having one day
gone to Clairvaulx, to see the most Blessed Abbot
Bernard, as he took leave with tears in his eyes,
he said, "I shall never see you again." But the
most holy Abbot comforted him with the promise
that he should see him once again.

William departed greatly consoled at the thought.
In A.D. 1153 on the night on which the most
Blessed Abbot passed away to the heavenly coun-
try, William being at Grandselve, the most holy

Bernard appeared to him during his sleep, and said, " Brother William." He answered, " Here I am, Reverend Father." The holy man added, " Come with me." He rose and went with him, and they walked together till they arrived at a very high mountain. Having reached this, the most reverend Father said to the Blessed William, " What place is this ?" But William answered, " I know not." The holy Bernard said to him, " This is the foot of the mysterious mountain of Libanus. You must remain here, whilst I ascend to the top of the mountain." William having asked him for what reason he was about to ascend, he answered, " that it was to learn things which he knew not." Upon which the Brother, much astonished, replied, " What is it you wish to learn, Reverend Father, and is there any one that knows more than you ?" The holy Father answered, " There is not here below any knowledge of the truth, it is up above that true knowledge alone exists." He then began to ascend the mountain, leaving the Brother at the foot, when of a sudden he awoke, with these words of the scripture on his tongue, " Blessed are the dead, who die in the Lord." He told the vision to his Abbot early in the morning. The Abbot remarked the day, and upon enquiry found that on that very day the most holy Father Bernard had quitted this earthly pilgrimage for the heavenly country.

The Blessed William died at Valdaune on the ninth of April, A.D. 1157.

William of Balada, an English Abbot, says,
that the only words of Latin known by this
Blessed man were " *Ave Maria.*" It is reported
that on his grave grew a lily, the petals of whose
flowers had written on them in letters of gold,
" *Ave Maria.*"

LIFE OF BLESSED ESKIL,

ARCHBISHOP OF LUND.

A GREAT man, and worthy of all reverence was
Blessed Eskil. Whilst yet a youth he was
sent to Saxony to study at Hildesheim. He there
fell into a grievous sickness, so that his life was
despaired of. As he grew worse he was anointed
with the holy oil. The Priests and people were
praying round him, when suddenly he seemed to
be in his last agony; his limbs relaxed, and he
appeared almost dead. His senses having left
him, he was led in spirit to a house which burned
within like a fiery oven. As he approached it,
desiring to behold, of a sudden the flames leaping
forth caught him unawares, and drew him unwillingly into the furnace of fire. As soon as he felt
the burning heat, he thought that there was nothing left for him but death and eternal fire. But
behold by the mercy of God he discovered a nar-
row path on one side of the house which appeared
free from flame, and led from door to door.
Gathering up his strength, he succeeded in making his way to this spot, and then passing quickly
from door to door, he fled with trembling and
beating heart from the face of the devouring fire.
Having escaped to the outside, he beheld before

him a large palace into which he entered, and
there on a throne of glory, with a countenance and
dress of wonderful beauty the Queen of the Angelic
choir was sitting. He approached her panting
with fear, and besought her to have pity on him.
She, beholding him with disdain, asked him in a
threatening manner how he dared to appear in her
sight, and bade him begone at once to the fire of
torment. Now amongst others near the throne
there stood also three venerable men whom he
recognized. One was the Bishop of the Church
where he dwelt, another the Dean, and the third a
certain Canon. The young man, therefore, turning to them, entreated of them to supplicate the
good Queen for him, which they accordingly did.
She, however, most merciful with sweet dissem-
bling, replied, " What is it that ye presume to ask
for this youth, so very vain and unworthy of my
regard? For in his perverse and slippery ways he
has never honoured me, nor once said my salutation." But when they besought her with her
wonted pitifulness to pass over the sins and igno-
rances of his youth if he would promise to amend,
the youth drew near and supplicated for himself
as follows : " O most pitiful Lady, have mercy
on me who dost not shut up thy bowels of compassion from any of the race of man, for I am
ready for the future to be thy servant, and after
God to venerate thee above all. If my father only
knew of my misfortune, he would be willing to
spend immense sums of gold for my deliverance."

With much simplicity he gave utterance to this
supplication. The Blessed among women looking
kindly on him, said: "And what thinkest thou is
a fitting price for thy redemption?"—"Oh,"
replied the youth, "anything rather than be sent
back any more into that fire of torment."—"I
will, then," she answered, "that thou render me
five measures of five different kinds of provisions,
that is, one of each." To which the youth with
all alacrity answered that he would gladly give
them, good measure, heaped up, and running over.
Those who had intercede for him became his
sureties, and he was let go to earth again.

Returning to himself, he sat up and broke into
a cry of joy, and said, "Blessed be God, I shall
no longer burn. I thank thee, holy Mother of
God, for having delivered me from this fire."
Those around him asked what had happened, but
he made no reply for some time, only saying,
"Thanks be to God." After a while, however,
he related the whole vision. A learned and good
man who was present, said to him, "You will
surely attain a high dignity in the Church of God,
and then you must erect five Monasteries of different Orders in honour of God and the holy Virgin
at your own expenses." The three persons whom
he saw in the vision died that same year.

In process of time Eskil was made Bishop of
Roskil, and obtained such a name for the sanctity
of his life that on the death of the Archbishop of
Lund, he was by the wish of the people made

11

Primate.   His election was opposed by King Eric, but he so won this monarch by the discreetness of his conduct as to overcome all opposition.   When raised to this dignity he took care for the fulfilment of his promise, and planted not five only, but many more Religious houses, among which were two of the Cistercian Observance, one from Citeaux, and the other from Clairvaulx.   He also took pains to root out the idolatrous rites, which still prevailed in some parts.

Having written to S. Bernard to obtain his influence in appeasing some disputes which had arisen, he conceived afterwards a great desire to see the Saint himself, and so determined to go to Clairvaulx.   On his return he received from the holy Abbot a loaf of bread to be kept in remem-brance of his visit.   The good Archbishop, fearing it would soon corrupt, desired to have it a second time baked in the oven, that being made very dry it might be preserved the better.   The holy Abbot chid him playfully for his want of faith, and said, " Think you that a blessing will not preserve the bread better than the baking of it ?"   He would not, therefore, let him take any but a common loaf, but blessed it, telling the Archbishop he need take no other precaution to prevent its corruption. The loaf kept quite fresh till he arrived after a long voyage by sea and land at his own home.

After ruling the See many years the holy old man resigned his Archbishopric, and ended his days as a Monk of Clairvaulx.

LIFE OF

THE BLESSED IDA OF LOUVAIN,

CISTERCIAN NUN.

IDA of Louvain was born of rich parents. Whilst she was but a very little girl, being taken to Church by her mother at the time of the elevation of the Host, she saw descending upon the altar a star of most brilliant lustre like a torch of lightning which shone for a few moments and then disappeared. This she told in a simple manner to her mother.

Her father was however a worldly man, and when Ida had reached her twenty-second year, she had to undergo from him a great storm of persecution on account of her piety. The foul fiend himself also used to persecute her by appearing visibly to her in the most horrible forms. Sometimes he shed around her a sweet odour, which was shortly after changed into a most dreadful stench. One night she saw a bier with a corpse upon it placed by her side. The maid however called quickly upon God, and the fantastical vision disappeared.

After this the Blessed Ida, at the time of the holy passion of the Lord, found that she had received also in her own body the same wounds which she had so much compassionated in that of our Lord. She at first tried to get them healed by outward appliances, but finding she could do nothing she strove only to hide them as much as she could. She suffered very great pains through these wounds, especially when persecuted by her father or others. She prayed however that our Lord would be pleased to remove these signs from her, and He graciously did so, but the same pains He caused her still to feel within.

Having gone one day to wash some corporals in a stream, a quantity of fish of all sorts came to her hands, playing, as it were, with her, and attaching themselves to her hands. She took some of them out of the water and put them on the plank on which she was kneeling, and after a while she put them again into the water, they playing around her till she took her leave of them.

Another time, when folding some corporals, and thinking of the loving kindness of the Lord, a fire was kindled within her which showed itself also by an external light, coming forth from her and shedding its splendour all around.

The Blessed Ida, when first she gave herself to God, lived alone in a cell walled up, adjoining the Church, but after some time she entered the Cistercian Abbey of the Valley of Roses. When she entered the Church there our Lord appeared to her bearing in His hand a crown of gold with many jewels, and amidst the jewels flowers of divers kinds. This He came and placed upon her head.

Now in the year of the probation the Novices were only allowed thrice during the whole period to receive the holy Sacrament of the Eucharist. When, however, the Nuns went to Communion, Ida used to go with them and receive the Communion also, no one seeing whether she were rendered invisible, and went in body, or whether she went through the spirit; certain it is that bodily as well as spiritually she was fed with the food of salvation. Her whole soul at these times melted away with divine love far more than when she made her ordinary sacramental Communion.

Another wonderful thing happened in the year of her probation. The holy maid was sick and laid up in the Infirmary. A Nun was given her as companion, who sat by her. One night when she was reading the Compline, and Ida was answering rather with the intense devotion of her heart than by alternate saying of the verses, the Nun who assisted her perceived a most exquisite odour to rise from the person of her sickly Sister, ascending to her nostrils, and penetrating with much abundance of sweetness into her whole frame. She felt in her mouth a strange savour, whose deliciousness exceeded that of honey or the honey-comb. It remained with her all that night and the day following. There was indeed in her mouth a liquid, like amber, which she had miraculously received from the Most High.

In the Monastery where the Blessed Ida lived, a Priest of the Cistercian Order was the Chaplain, who once in anger cast forth injurious words against the spouse of God. He sent for her to beg her pardon, but she refused to come, still bearing somewhat of a grudge in her mind. Next day he was saying Mass according to his office, and Ida was behind at his feet, when of a sudden she was rapt in ecstasy and saw herself clothed in the priestly vestments, and so going through the Mass was renewed with the sacrament of the Lord's Body. In this vision she lost all thought of the Priest, neither adverting to his presence in body or mind. On that day he sent for her again, and she no longer delayed to come, for the Lord had brought His two chosen ones to one by the reception of His own most sacred Body and Blóod. Forgetting altogether the wrong done her she went to him at once, and as she opened the secrets of her conscience she told him how the day before she had received the Body of the Lord, and what marvels God had wrought in her.

Another time, when she purposed to receive the sacred Food of life, she was going towards the altar, when she suddenly bethought her that, going to such a Feast, she ought to be accompanied by some escort. This made her pause, and as the Priest looked towards her to know why she did not approach, he saw, and lo! at her right hand appeared the lovely Queen of virgins, and at her left the disciple whom Jesus loved, escorting her towards the altar, an Angel going before, strewing the way with sweetest incense and holding a light also. As she returned from Communion, they in like manner led her back to her place.

On a certain day, after having been to Confession, and as she was preparing herself in quiet for the sacred Communion, she was suddenly called to go to speak to a Friar Minor, who had come from Mechlin to see her. Very unwillingly she obeyed, and going to him she sat down and addressed him a few words and then was silent. Now turning her eyes away from him they caught sight of another Friar, his companion, who was waiting outside in the snow. She had never seen him before, and she looked full at him, and laughed aloud, at the same time raising her eyes up in a manner quite unusual with her, and gazing at him to the wonder of all.

Now the Priest who had heard her Confession was in the same place, hearing those of others. He, beholding her from a distance, and being shocked at the boldness of her gaze, especially for the scandal that might be given to others, rebuked her for it, but she, not paying any attention, kept her eyes still fixed full upon that Brother. After some while she turned her eyes away, spoke to the other Friar a few words to satisfy his devotion, and then both went into the Church. All that day till evening she tasted nothing, and then could only be induced to take a little by great urgency, for she had been quite overcome by the sweetness which had overwhelmed her, when she had received the Sacred Host, and instead of going with the rest back to her place, she had remained almost in ecstasy behind the altar till after Sext, and had then gone to the Infirmary. That evening, when another Nun was present, the Priest again rebuked her for her behaviour before those Friars, asking her why she laughed. She answered, "She could not help doing so, seeing that that Brother was a vessel of the Lord, full of great gifts of the Spirit of God." Then she added, "that sometimes she felt so full of light that she could see the secrets of all hearts;" and turning to the Priest himself, she said, "Your own state is known to me. Keep yourself in solitude of mind and silence of spirit, and avoid outward occupations, lest you be stript of the gift of divine grace, and be left destitute of spiritual goods."

Among other graces which the handmaid of God received, one is worthy of being noticed. Oftentimes a brilliant light issued from her eyes, like a ray of the sun. This happened especially when she had been given to drink of the Blood of the Lord. The Priest sometimes thought the beams of the sun were shining on the chalice, but, on closer observation, found the light to come from the eyes of the Virgin of Christ. Once, when she was keeping watch near the Ciborium, another Nun observed a great light, and through curiosity went close up to her to observe where it

came from, when, as Ida turned her face half
veiled towards her, she saw that this brilliant
splendour came from her eyes, which shone like
lamps of fire.

On the vigil of Saint Michael, having finished
her own vesper in the Infirmary, Ida went out
into the open court that she might hear the voices
of the Nuns in choir. Hearing them, her own
heart also was filled with the spirit of praise,
hymning in spirit with the Angels the glories of
the Creator. As she reached the wall on the
East, she was quite overcome, and falling into an
ecstasy of mind was lifted up into the heavenly
Court to the choir of the Seraphs, who are nearest
to the majestic presence of God. There in amazed
awe she beheld the excellent glory of the light of
God, which was beyond all that man can utter or
even can conceive.

On the festival of Saint John Baptist being in
the choir of the sick, when with deep devotion the
Nuns were singing the *Sanctus* in the Choir, the
holy Ida was in the spirit, and beheld in excess of
mind how to each of the Sisters a beautiful crown
was given, wrought by Angelic hands, for the
sweet concert of musical voices that had been presented before the Most High God. These circlets
of gold were placed on the head of each as the
reward they should have for ever, if only they
should so persevere to the end.

Ida, herself, also received a crown at the same
time, of not less beauty and elegance than the

rest; the other sick, however, received none, as they were not joining in praise. Many other great gifts and graces did the Blessed Ida receive, which it would be too long to narrate. Having fulfilled her course, she passed away from earth, fortified with the sacraments of holy Church, on the thirteenth day of April, and as some say, in the year of our Lord 1200.

LIFE OF SAINT FRANCIA,

ABBESS OF PECTOLA.

THE Blessed Francia was born at Piacenza, in Italy, in the year of our Lord 1173, of the illustrious family of the Counts of Vidalta. As soon as her mind began to open, her letters were taught her, and her parents taught her the way of virtue. When she was seven years old she pronounced her intention of renouncing the world, in order to serve Jesus Christ free from all other engagements, for even at this age all her thoughts were of religion. Her father placed her at once in a Monastery, that her young heart might run no danger of being corrupted by the world. He chose for this end that of Saint Cyrus of the Order of Saint Benedict. She remained there till fourteen years of age as a Novice, rendering herself agreeable to God by her manners so pure and staid, her exactitude to all the observances, and her whole general behaviour. She then made her profession, and being about to receive the veil from the hands of the Bishop of Piacenza, there appeared an Angel, who took it and placed it on her head. After her profession she contented herself in Lent with dry bread, to which at most she added some raw herbs, without any seasoning of the most simple kind, such as salt or water. She ate nothing that was cooked. This kind of diet injured her stomach, but she would use nothing to relieve herself, nor take any medicines.

At the age of twenty-three, the Nuns chose her for their Abbess. No long time, however, after this, a Nun who was a sister of the Bishop of Piacenza, contrived to raise a number of the Nuns against her, and the Bishop showed himself favourable to them. She held her tongue, however, and bore patiently with their malice, waiting only an opportunity of resigning her Office, and leaving the Convent.

An opportunity soon offered. A young person of high family having retired into the Monastery in the year of grace 1212, she counselled her to take the habit in a Monastery of the Order of Citeaux, near Genoa, named Rapalla, and then to build with her dowry a Monastery of that Order. This advice the young girl, named Carenza, followed. After the Noviciate was over, she returned to consult with Francia. They chose for the new establishment a solitary place on the top of a mountain, called Lana, some distance from Piacenza.

When the Monastery was finished, Francia, with nine of the Nuns of Saint Cyrus, and Carenza the foundress, entered the new Monastery, placing themselves at once under the Order of Citeaux. The Abbot of Colomba, in the diocese of Piacenza, clothed them with the habit, he taking the new

Convent as the daughter of his Abbey. The Blessed Francia was made Abbess, and Carenza, Prioress. This happened in the year of grace 1214.

The Nuns of Saint Cyrus were not well pleased at the departure of the Blessed Francia. They now saw the value of her whom they had lost. Not being able to bring her back again, they kept up a continual correspondence with her, living according to her counsels. The new Monastery was, however, found in some ways so inconvenient that, after two years' residence in it, the Nuns removed to Valeria. This Monastery being, however, in the town, did not content them, and two years later they received a retired house, called Pectola, where they built a Church, and placed it under the invocation of the most holy Virgin Mary. Here they lived till, on account of the wars, they were forced to retire for safety to Piacenza. This Monastery was well provided for, inasmuch as a number both of Virgins and Widows had sought refuge there, bringing with them a large portion of worldly wealth.

The holy Mother Francia gave herself to God with more closeness than ever, and the days not sufficing her, she watched far into the night, before the altar of Saint Michael, for whom she had a special veneration. Carenza the Prioress, and some other Nuns, seeing that their holy Abbess became exhausted with her long watches, thought to hinder her from undertaking them by locking the doors of the Church at the time she was accustomed to enter it. The holy Mother finding the doors locked, and suspecting who had done it, turned to Jesus Christ, and said, " What,. Lord ! do my own children, whom I try to unite to my own Spouse, try to snatch You away from me, a thing which the demons cannot do ? Are they envious of me ?" She had scarce finished these words, when the doors opened of their own accord, and gave her free entrance into the Church.

In order to prevent sleep stealing upon her in these nightly watches, the holy Mother had a machine made, on which her hands were stretched into the form of a cross. It was so arranged that, if her arms at all sank down, she received strokes from above, so as effectually to wake her up again. The Enemy of mankind, unable to injure her soul, vented his rage sometimes upon her body. One day, when she was at prayer, she received from him so rude a stroke in the mouth, that her teeth were broken, and her whole face swelled up. She, however, with great patience, remained at her prayer in the same place, which so enraged the malignant fiend, that he made a deep wound in one of her feet, and she could not move for a long time, till it gradually was healed.

Towards the middle of Lent, in the year of grace 1218, the Blessed Francia was seized with pains in her stomach, that caused her the greatest anguish. The Prioress, seeing that the fever increased upon her day by day, obtained of her by urgent prayers, that she would allow some roots to be served her, cooked, contrary to her usual Lenten habitude. When she saw these cooked vegetables before her, she raised her eyes and her heart to God, praying full earnestly that she might know His will, and whether, on account of the violence of her pain, she ought to eat them, or to abstain from them in the spirit of penance. And when she had raised the knife and begun to cut what lay before her, blood gushed out upon the knife for an evident token, that it was the will of God she should not eat of them.

Then she spoke to her Nuns, and said, " My children, it is hard for you to kick against the goad. God in His mercy has made me suffer in this life what I should have had to suffer in the next. I might give up my abstinence, but I could not lessen my sufferings, for who can resist the will of God? You tried to hinder me in my watchings, but it was useless, and now you have tried to relax the rigour of my fasts, but you have not succeeded better. Do not then for the future make useless efforts, but leave me in the hands of my God. Bodily remedies are of no avail in the sicknesses sent by God, for the healing of the wounds of our souls. And indeed, if they could relieve me, it were not good, ' because these pains will deliver me from the sufferings of the next life.' " Having finished these words, she signed herself with the sign of the cross, and immediately she felt better.

When Easter was come, which in that year fell
on the fifteenth of April, she sent for her Nuns,
feeling that her end was not far off.   As they
entered her chamber, she said, "With great desire
have I desired to eat this Pasch with you before I
die."   The Nuns all burst into tears at these
words.   She comforted them as well as she could,
exhorting them to be evermore faithful to their
rule.   All that day was passed in conversation
with one or other, and in tears.   As the holy
Mother grew worse she sent word to the Abbot of
Colomba to come.   To him she made her last
Confession, receiving from him the last sacraments of religion.   She gave up her precious soul
into the hands of her spouse the twenty-fifth day
of April, 1218.   She was then forty-three years
of age.   Her body was buried opposite the altar
of S. Michael, in the place where she used to
pray.

The Lord God, however, willing the more to
glorify His handmaiden, the Blessed Francia appeared to a certain Cistercian Monk, with two
Martyrs, whilst he was at prayer, revealing to him
the great glory God had given her for her labours.
Saint Michael also, the Archangel, charged him in
a vision to have the body of the Blessed Francia
translated from its resting place to some more
honourable place.   The Monk, considering that it
was but a vision, paid no heed to it, but an angel
again appearing, told him he should be dumb till
he had fulfilled the command.   The Monk then,

unable to speak, made known by writing what had happened. The body of the Blessed Francia was accordingly elevated, and was found entirely incorrupt. It was translated to a more honourable resting-place, where many miracles were wrought by her intercession.

LIFE OF BLESSED JOHN,

PRIOR OF CLAIRVAULX.

THE Blessed John, many years Prior of Clairvaulx, was a man of wonderful fervour, who
discharged all the duties of his office with great
fidelity.

He assisted at the work of God with a lively
and ardent devotion, never dispensing himself
from it neither day nor night. He paid particular
attention to the psalms, which were sung with a
manly vigorous voice. All admired his exactitude
and care, but few were capable of imitating him.
He had received from his Creator a loud strong
voice, which he used with great power and zeal in
singing His praises, from whom He received this
gift. He set continually before his eyes the choirs
of the Angels in the court of heaven, and in concert with them he offered before the Divine Majesty the sacrifice of prayer and praise.

That he might not give way to sleep during the
long psalmody of the night, he had contrived to
make a hammer of wood in such a fashion as that
it should strike him if from sleepiness he did not
hold his head erect.

At labour, which he loved much, he encouraged

greatly all the Brethren both by word and example. Especially he exhorted them by the harvest
labours under a burning sun to blot out by penance all the negligences of the past year.

He had a great dislike of new clothing, especially such as was fine or costly, and rather desired
what had been patched and mended.

Any indulgence to him was extremely painful.
It required a very pressing necessity to make him
use it, especially to be absent from Vigils, or to
go to the Infirmary. It came to pass one night
that he could not chant the psalms with his usual
power. His pain increasing, he for a long time
resisted his desire to leave the Church. The
office over, he retired apart in sadness, fearing he
would be obliged to go to the Infirmary. "Ah!"
said he, talking with himself, "what shall we do
now? What is going to happen to us? What!
have you fallen sick at last? And are you going
to let yourself be driven to the Infirmary by a
little thing like this? Are you going to give up
your penance, and lose its reward? Come! trust
in God! He is powerful enough to soothe your
pain without your giving up your penance."

The Blessed John, however, was overheard by a
Brother, who happened to be near, and he went to
inform Saint Gerard, the Abbot, who had much
difficulty in persuading him to consent to go to
the Infirmary, though his illness had become
grave. When he was in his last sickness, Eskil,
Archbishop of Loudun, and Alan, Bishop of

Auxerre, came to see him, and out of compassion would have given him finer clothing to wear, but he consented not, fearing the judgment of God.

He put off the burden of the flesh in the year of our Lord 1179, on the twelfth day of November.

LIFE OF SAINT STEPHEN,

ABBOT OF OBAZINE.

THE Father of this Blessed man was named Stephen, like himself, and was of the country of Limoges. He, with his wife Guanberte, lived without reproach in the sight of God and men.

Guanberte, being great with child, dreamed that she gave birth to a little white dog, that had the keeping of a flock of sheep, the Lord thus signifying that her son was to be a great pastor of souls in His Church.

The young Stephen, when yet of tender age, was sent to be educated in letters by persons well learned in all wisdom, and he advanced with rapid step both in science and godliness. His father having died, he became in his stead as a father to his mother and to his brethren, being prudent and discreet in the discharge of the affairs of the family. He exercised great hospitality towards the poor, being the right hand of the widow and orphan, and keeping himself in all things unspotted from the world.

Such was his life before it pleased God to call him to the Office of the Priesthood, when, as it were by a new conversion, he gave his heart more

closely to God than before, taking care to wear no
clothing but what was coarse and simple, and eating no food but what was plain and homely. He
kept his body in subjection with hair cloth, and
sometimes would break the ice in a pond, and
enter into the water up to the neck, remaining
there till the cold had pierced every part of his
body. To this he added an almost continual fast,
weeping with many sighs and tears, in a spirit of
penance.

He had a great gift for preaching the Word of
God, and people were never tired of hearing the
words of wisdom which flowed from his lips. In
all his conversation with others his words were
seasoned with salt, and had about them a holy
unction and a fire, which kindled the hearts of
those who heard him with the love of God. His
whole life was that of one devoted to God. The
Church Offices were his delight. Nothing but
grievous sickness could keep him from assisting
at them. He took care that everything for the
service of God's altar should be exceeding clean
and fair. His reading was in the divine scriptures, but especially in the study of the Gospels.
It was in these books that he learnt those maxims
which taught him the vanity of all earthly things,
and withdrew him at last entirely from the com-
merce of the world.

The Blessed Stephen would do nothing however
indiscreetly, but, lest he might be deceived by the
arch Enemy through the appearance of good, he

determined to go first to a man of God abiding in those parts, and who bore the same name as himself. This holy man advised him by no means to put off his conversion from the world, for that what he had conceived in his mind was from the Holy Ghost. This counsel he at once set about fulfilling, keeping secret his design from all except one Peter, a close companion of his, who also resolved to accompany him.

At the beginning of Lent they distributed to the poor all the goods of which they were possessed; and then, after passing the whole previous night in prayer, in the early morning they put on the habit of a Hermit, and casting their shoes, went forth from their own country to search a place of abode in the solitude.

They first went and placed themselves under the guidance of a Hermit, named Bertrand, who had a few disciples living with him in a desert place. After staying with him ten months, it seemed to them that the life was not hard enough, and they left him to seek for a place more wild and solitary, where they might do penance to their hearts' desire. After some search they discovered a spot, shut in on all sides by overhanging rocks, which seemed ever about to fall, and wholly covered with briars and thorns. Into this frightful desert they went still further on with naked feet, and on Good Friday and the following day they ate nothing whatsoever. When Easter was come, going to a Church not far off, one of them offered the holy Sacrifice, giving the sacred Communion to the other. This done, they prayed awhile, and returned to their desert, having found no one to give them anything to eat. As, however, they sat on the side of a hill, worn out with the weariness of the way, a certain woman from a neighbouring village gave them half a loaf and a pot of milk, which they received in their necessity with great thanksgiving of heart.

God, however, was pleased severely to try the patience of His servants, and for this end allowed them to be so neglected, that for food they had for a long time nothing but the wild herbs and roots which the desert land produced of itself. Occasionally, the shepherds of the neighbourhood would bring them a little present, and once a charitable man, who was carrying some provisions for the poor, lost his way on the road, and at last, to his surprise, came up to the abode of these two hermits. He gave them sufficient to last them two entire days. Their ordinary food was the wild roots and the leaves of trees.

They began however now to clear the ground a little, and to till it for their own use. Another clergyman, named Bernard, had joined himself to their company. Desiring to have the approval of the Bishop, Stephen sent to him, to Limoges, his disciple Peter and the above named Bernard. The Bishop Eustonge was well content with what was told him and bade them persevere. He also gave permission to build a Monastery, and to celebrate there the Holy Sacrifice. Several others now came to join them. This was the manner of life they followed. With the exception of the time marked out for Office and reading, the day was passed in labour. They ate but once a day towards evening. Almost all the night they passed in prayer, giving but a short time to sleep, after which they rose for the Vigils of the night. Whatever time remained was given to labour till the morning light. Then they said Prime, after which followed the Mass, and then they went out to labour.

The Blessed Stephen remained in the house to perform the office of cook, getting ready the vegetables, cutting and bringing in the wood for firing, washing up the vessels used at table, and doing all other things of the service of the kitchen.

Nevertheless he kept a strict watch over the Brethren, punishing them faithfully if they committed any faults, such as raising the eyes in Church, giving way to laughter, making a noise, or falling half asleep. He also formed them to such a silence, that the sound of their voice was never heard. Their fame began to spread abroad, and men admired the wonderful life that these angelic men had reached to.

Now, as time went on, the band of men who put themselves under the guidance of the Blessed Stephen became more and more numerous, and the desert became a place of much resort. This did not please him, nay, it became an insupport-

able burden. He had left the world, but the world
had come after him, and would not leave him.
He cast in his mind what he might do to escape,
and it appeared to him a good counsel to go away
into the country of the Saracens, and there give
his life to martyrdom for Jesus Christ. He hoped
that his friend Peter would be of the same mind.
Peter, however, would not listen to him at all on
this matter. On the contrary, he told him plainly
that he thought it a deceit of the Wicked One,
and by no means an aspiration from the Most
High. The Blessed man yielded to his reasons,
and determined that his martyrdom should be in
the middle of France, in a life spent for the salvation of the souls of his own countrymen.

After this they sought out a place, where they
might conveniently build a Monastery, which so
enraged the spirit of evil, that he appeared in a
visible form to one of the workmen, and inflicted
grievous injuries upon him. Seeing, however,
that the work still went on, he then, during the
night, attacked the Blessed Stephen himself.
This he did often, till at last the servant of God,
unable to sleep, caused some of the Brethren to
recite psalms in his chamber for the confusion
of the Evil One, whilst he should take a little
repose.

The buildings being finished, a contest arose
between Stephen and his friend Peter, who should
take the command. Each one putting forward the
claims of the other. At last they agreed to refer

the matter to the Legate of the Holy See, who, setting aside the reasons Stephen gave why Peter should be Superior, commanded the Blessed man to undertake the charge himself.

The same observance was carried on as before. They fasted all the year except the Sundays of Paschal time. In winter, when the nights were long, they assembled after Complin, and worked till half the Psalter was said through. They always said Psalms or other prayers during their work.

Having heard of the holy conversation of the Carthusian Friars, the man of God desired much to visit them. He therefore determined to go with two of his Brethren to their Monastery. It was the middle of winter, and he made the journey on foot, the roads being covered with ice and snow, and his feet often being naked, with no shoes to protect them. As they journeyed on, he recited psalms with his companions. Having arrived at the Grande Chartreuse, the Prior received them with great courtesy. Seeing the perfection of these Monks, the Blessed man desired to put himself and the Brethren with him under their rule, but the Prior counselled him rather to go to Citeaux, as a more suitable observance, and one eminently holy.

When he was returned to his Monastery, he began to build a new Church for the Brethren on the model of that of the Carthusians, the one then in use being quite too small for their number.

Near to the Monastery he built also another for
guests and strangers that they might not, by entering the Church of the Brethren, in any way trouble
their repose. When there was any difficulty in
raising the stones, the Blessed man made the sign
of the cross, and presently the weight of the stone
seemed gone, and all difficulties passed away.

After this Monastery was finished, another was
added some little distance off for women, who
should renounce the world. A number of ladies,
delicately brought up, did so. They embraced
with gladsome mind the poverty of the cross, and
had more joy in wearing their coarse, vile habits,
than formerly they had in their raiment of silk
and gold. They took more delight in the work of
the kitchen than formerly in adorning themselves
with luxuries in their magnificent chambers.

It was shortly after this that, consulting with
the Bishop of Limoges, Stephen came to the resolution of joining the Order of Citeaux. In order
to do this he invited certain Monks of the Abbey
of Dalon to come and preside in his Monastery,
and teach to the Brethren the observances of the
Cistercian Order. This was accordingly done,
though not altogether to the satisfaction of the
Brethren, for new customs were difficult to learn,
and their new masters rather rude and rash in
their corrections.

His Monks, however, being now sufficiently instructed, the Blessed Stephen took his journey to
Citeaux, in the year of Redemption 1148, in that

year when the Pope Eugenius the third assisted at the great Chapter of the Order. The Pope received him with a most kind welcome, and approved of his desire to place his Monasteries under the Order of Citeaux. He then brought him before Rainard, Abbot of Citeaux, who himself, taking him into the Chapter of the assembled Fathers, said to them, "You see here an Abbot, neither imposing in stature nor grand in appearance, but it is a man filled with faith, and with the Spirit of God." When the Chapter was over the man of God returned to Obazine with five Monks of Citeaux, who might teach the Brethren more exactly all the points of the Cistercian Observance. They obliged them to write out again all the books of the Divine Office and Chant, the whole of them having been lately revised by the great Father Saint Bernard, and some other skilled persons amongst the Brethren. Another thing was the usage of flesh meat, which the man of God had not, up to that time, permitted even to the sick. This he was still much averse to, saying that the house of God was being turned into a butcher's shop. When, however, the Chapter of the Rule was shown to him, he held his peace, not willing to sanction, yet unwilling to condemn.

The Brethren still multiplying, he built two new Monasteries, one in the diocese of Cahors, the other in that of Xaintes, and he had also to build larger structures for the accommodation of his own Monks.

The Bishop of Limoges came to lay the first
stone of the new buildings, together with the
architect and the Blessed man of God himself.
On that day a great crowd both of the gentlemen
of those parts and of the poor assembled for the
ceremony, and a collection of money was made for
the expenses of the buildings. The Bishop wished
the same to be made on the other days, but the
man of God withstood him, although the Bishop
promised to give Indulgences to those who should
give alms. "No," said the holy man. "We do
not wish to be a scandal to others and a confusion
to ourselves, by going on all sides showing the
graces we bestow, and Indulgences which we have
no power of according. Our sins lie heavy on us,
how can we dare to take upon us to bear those of
others also?" The Bishop hearing this answer
was greatly consoled, being assured that he was
now dealing with a true servant of God, filled with
His holy fear.

Whilst the Brethren were occupied in building,
a great famine came, and the people were brought
down to the last extremity. Stephen, placing all
his trust in God, hired a great number of men as
labourers. So great was the demand for bread,
that they were obliged to bake the oven full two or
three times every day. Besides the bread he gave
all that was laid up in the store rooms. He
wished also those on the farms to do the like.
One day, when a Brother told him he had nothing
left for the Monks or the poor, he replied, "If you

have no bread kill the cattle, keeping only those that serve for the plough. But if those are not enough, kill them all, that the poor may not starve." The Brother returned to execute these orders, having only a provision of corn for three days, and began to distribute it to the poor. The Lord God, however, so multiplied the remains, that it sufficed both for the poor and for the wants of the Brethren till the harvest came in.

One day the Father Steward came to the man of God who was sick, and seemed lost with sadness, so that he could scarce speak. Upon being asked what was the matter, he answered, at last, " Alas! my Father, the Brethren will not be able to dine to-day, there is no bread in the house, and now is the dinner hour." The holy man, lifting up his eyes after his wont, said, " What, Brother, is the hand of God then shortened so that He cannot give us bread? Because you have none, you fancy that He has none to give us. Go and prepare the tables as usual. Trust in God. I do not believe He will leave His servants without their daily bread." The Steward did as he was told, and as the Brethren were going in to dinner, there came a man bringing some horses, loaded with panniers of bread, which had been sent by some good people in those parts.

It came to pass that there was once a dispute between the Viscount of Turenne and another Lord named William. It arose in this manner. William had got possession of a Falcon, which

had been let loose by the Viscount, and refused to
give it up. The Viscount, considering this a great
insult, threatened that he would lay waste all his
lands.   Now some people took one side, and some
took the other, and the whole province was about
to join battle. William, thinking this a good
occasion for seizing on the lands of the Viscount,
far from sending back the falcon, delivered it for
safer keeping into the hand of one of his friends,
who lived at a distance.

The Blessed Stephen could not bear to see the
whole country at war for such a trifle. He went
to the Viscount, and besought him to desist, but
seeing he gained nothing, he at last prevailed on
him to do so, provided he would bring back to
him the lost falcon.   Then throwing himself into
the midst of the troops, he commanded them by
the authority of the Viscount to return home.
Having been to William, and learning where the
falcon was, he went off to search for the man who
detained it.   This man being informed of the
object of his journey, not only refused to give it
up, but covered the Blessed man with insults, and
had him driven out of the place.

Tired and worn, he was glad to find refuge in
the house of a poor labourer near the town, having eaten nothing that day. The next day he
went again in search of the man who had so abused
him. His Brethren who accompanied him sought
to dissuade him. He however said that this man
was no longer the same man as yesterday. And,

indeed, so it was; for being in bed when the Blessed Stephen arrived, and hearing that he was come, he got at once from his bed, and ran with naked feet to cast himself prostrate before him, in the midst of a public place covered with snow, begging humbly that he would pardon the affronts of which he had been guilty, and rendering back the bird into his hands. The man of God raised him from the ground with great courtesy, received the bird from his hands, and taking his leave, brought it to the Viscount of Turenne, and so restored peace.

The Blessed Stephen having sent a Monk named Aimery on a journey for some affairs of the Monastery, he dismounted for a time from his mule in order to spare it a little. No sooner had he done so than it escaped from his hands, and fled away. He and his companion ran after it, but in vain did they attempt to come up with it. At last, in despair of any other method, the Brother called with a loud voice, " I command you, under pain of obedience, and by the merits of our holy Father, not to go any further, but to wait till I come up to you." At these words the mule stopped till the Brother came up, and quietly allowed himself to be taken. " Ha !" said the Brother to his companion, " how great is the virtue of obedience, which even the dumb beasts respect and honour."

Another Brother was once drawing wine, when one came and signed to him that the Blessed

13

Father Stephen desired his presence. He went off at once, leaving the barrel running. Having fulfilled that for which he was sent, he returned in haste, remembering that he had left the tap of the barrel open, and supposing the wine would be all run away. He was astonished to find that though his vessel was full, not a drop more had run out of the barrel.

There was nothing about the man of God by nature, that could render him pleasing in the eyes of others, but from the beauty of the inward man there flowed forth such a grace over the exterior, that people were never weary of looking at him. The most trifling of his actions such as were done without any reflection, had something pleasing and edifying in them. His manners were so courteous, so agreeable, and his words so full of sense, that all were captivated by the charm of his conversation and presence. No one was more mild in ordinary matters, no one more severe when the glory of God was at stake. Thus he was loved and feared at the same time. A little look from him made such an impression on the heart, for he seemed to know its most hidden secrets, and to pierce its inmost folds. Even his smile, though so grateful, had something in it which repressed familiarity, and engendered reverence. To all this he joined a great simplicity, judging well of others, and always hoping the best.

Although the chief over the Brethren, he conducted matters rather by charity than by autho-

rity, remembering the words of Jesus Christ,
"Let him that is greatest among you be as the
least, and him that ruleth be as him that serveth."
He had such consideration and respect for all, that
he feared to give them the smallest pain, when he
saw they submitted to his authority.   If they
committed faults, he rebuked them plainly and
simply ; severely also if necessary, but mingling
sweetness with his reproof.   Thus he made himself so beloved, that it was a great sorrow to the
Brethren, when he had to go on a journey, and it
was like a feast for them to behold his return.
For, indeed, he was a good Father to them,
strengthening the weak, sustaining those that
wanted courage, comforting the afflicted, providing
for their necessities either of body or soul ; slack-
ing the too great fervour of some, and pushing on
others to do more.   To some it was sufficient reproof to let them know that he was not ignorant
of their faults, for he knew this very thing would
cover them with confusion, and cause them to
amend.   Others he punished in the most severe
manner.

There was a certain Monk, who was always asking permission to go out of the Monastery, a permission which the Blessed Father knew to be very
inexpedient for him.   At last, seeing that he evermore persisted in the same request, he gave him
leave, provided first he should receive a good discipline.   The Monk having agreed to this he had
a discipline given to him, so severe and so long,

that the devil who tempted him was entirely driven out. Scarcely was the discipline over than the Brother cried out that now he had no longer any wish to go out. "My temptation," he said, "is so entirely passed away, that I have not the slightest wish ever to leave the Monastery, as long as I live."

A like example to this occurs in the life of S. Peter Damian.

So exact was he that no unseemly gesture could escape his reproof. If they made a noise in walking, or in eating, they were sure of being chidden for it. To spit in an unseemly way, to yawn, or speak a word out of place, he suffered not to pass without correction, so that his Monks were known at once by their modest look, full of religion, their grave step and downcast eyes, their seemly speech, all perfect and worthy of the majesty of the disciples of Jesus Christ.

It is said that a lady once, seeing some Monks passing along at a little distance, remarked of them, that assuredly they did not belong to the Monastery of Obazine. Their mien and their gestures were wanting in that seemly perfection which was the characteristic of the Brethren of Obazine.

When the Ministers of the Altar were dressing, he himself arranged their vestments, taking care that all might be adjusted with the greatest propriety, and that nothing might appear out of keeping with the holiness of those sacred Mysteries. When he himself went to the Altar, although he wore his Cowle, it was so arranged underneath his priestly vestments as not in any way to interfere with the comeliness of their appearance. He also took care that the altars should be properly covered, the cloth hanging equally on all sides, and no dust or any other indecency in the house of God.

The days now came when it was time for the Blessed man to shift off this mortal coil. He laboured, however, to the last. The Abbot of one of his Monasteries, of which he had founded several of both sexes, had gone the way of all flesh, and he took his journey thither, to preside at the choosing of another. Whilst there he was taken with a fever, tidings of which soon reached Obazine, and the Brethren were in consternation. All work ceased. They could do nothing but sob and weep. It seemed like a Good Friday, so silent and still was the whole house, the Monks moving about like shadows.

Some of the Brethren went to Bonnaique, the Abbey where the holy old man lay sick. He received them with the greatest tenderness, giving them his blessing. They were inconsolable at the thought of losing his sweet presence. "Ah!" they said, in their anguish of heart, "why do you leave us, Father? To whose hands do you entrust us? However poor we might be, yet with you with us we were rich, having you as our guide and pastor. But now what shall we do? Whither shall we turn in our affliction?"

He tried to comfort them as well as he could, begging them to pray for him, and promising that he would assist them as far as he could. He also exhorted them to keep faithfully up to the rule, and to observe all its statutes and ordinances. After he had received the last Sacraments of the Church, the Brethren began to say the prayers for those in their last agony, in which, though ready to expire, he joined audibly. Then, as a last thing, one of the Brethren guiding and supporting his hand, he gave his blessing to the Monastery, and breathed forth his spirit on the sixth of March, A.D. 1159.

It was about midnight that he passed, being the second Sunday of Lent. His body was clothed in his priestly Vestments, and thus carried to the Church. On Sunday morning all the Masses were said for him, and then without further delay the body was carried forth from the Church by his Monks on the way to Obazine. A great number of Abbots, Monks, Clergy, and laymen, chanting psalms, went before, and followed after in procession. An immense crowd gathered along the road, and as they passed by any Church the body was carried in to receive from the priests the absolutions of the dead, all the bells ringing, and the censers waving. The Countess of Provence was healed of a malady, that had a long time tormented her, and various other cures were wrought during the passage of the body of the holy old man. The Countess wished that the body might rest the night in one of her Churches, but the Brethren, fearing she might wish to retain it, would not consent. The night was passed, therefore, on a farm, in the middle of the road, a place having been prepared whereon to rest the body, and such a number of lights being lit round it that it seemed as light as day. All night long the Clergy in Copes chanted psalms, and the Monks succeeded one another in these pious duties of charity. The night being passed, with the early dawn they were again on the road.

Meanwhile, the Monks of Obazine, learning early on Monday morning what was being done, themselves, after Mass was over, went forth to meet their Father's funeral corse. Oh what weepings and lamentations, and cries of sorrow were there, when at last they saw the funeral company coming along. And when they met them, and all paused for awhile, what sobs burst from their anguished hearts and what tears ran down their cheeks, and they kissed and kissed again the dear hand of him they had so loved, whose voice they should never hear again in this mortal frame. For he was, after God, all their joy and all their consolation.

It was verging towards night when they reached Obazine. There Gerard, Abbot of one of the daughter houses of Obazine, with several of his Monks, met them. He it was that should perform the last rites of absolution. Overcome with grief he fell senseless over the bier. Then again broke forth loud cries of woe from their rent hearts. There was no dry eye there. This Abbot, being at last brought to himself, finished the ceremony as well as he could.

All Tuesday the body lay exposed to the veneration of the people, and the Almighty hand was shown in various cures wrought upon those who had touched the body. On Wednesday, with great solemnity, the body was laid in a grave in the Chapter. For many years after, offerings of wax lights and of lamps were made to be burnt at his tomb, these being the tokens of gratitude given by those who had received miraculous favours from his hand.

LIFE OF BLESSED ROBERT,

SECOND ABBOT OF CLAIRVAULX.

AFTER the holy Father Bernard, escaping from the prison-house of the body, had taken his flight to the mansion prepared for him among the citizens of heaven, by a common desire of the Brethren, Robert of Dunes was elected Abbot of Clairvaulx. He was a native of Bruges, being kinsman to the holy Father Bernard according to the flesh. From him, as a faithful disciple, he drank in those lessons of holiness for which he became afterwards so illustrious. Even from his earliest years he had given proofs to the world of a singular goodness, which he afterwards the more confirmed by the angelical sanctity of his whole life.

Burning with desire for perfection, he, together with the noble Geoffrey of Perona, enrolled his name in the Abbey of Clairvaulx, whence, after having given there for some years an admirable example of virtue, he was sent to Flanders to lay the foundation of the holy Cistercian Observance at Dunes. This Monastery had been founded many years before by the Blessed Liger, who lived as a Hermit in its neighbourhood.

Abbot Fulco was its second Abbot, receiving the

holy habit of Religion from the. Blessed Liger himself, who belonged to the Order of Savigni. Fulco, with all his Monks, when the fame of the Blessed Bernard and of the new Cistercian Order came to their ears, one and all laying aside the habit and customs of their own Order, embraced the Observance of Citeaux. Fulco also resigned his dignity of Abbot, and in his place was instituted the Blessed Robert. This took place in the Chapter at Clairvaulx, in the month of April, A.D. 1138.

Robert then left Clairvaulx, not indeed without shedding many tears. In these tears this disciple was joined by his loving Master the holy Bernard, and they wept together at their unhappy separation. But as he parted in sorrow from those of Clairvaulx, so was he received with great gladness by the Monks of Dunes. He had not been long in his new home, when he received from the Abbot Bernard an epistle, testifying his great love towards him. It runs as follows : " To my dearly beloved Brother and friend, the Abbot Robert, Brother Bernard of Clairvaulx. My dearly loved Robert, too late were you known to me, and too soon taken from me ; but I am consoled, for I only suffer the loss of your bodily presence, being in spirit ever with you. But even this loss, how could I endure it with even mind, were it not that I know God has caused it ? There will, however, come a day when we shall be restored to one another, and we shall then be able to rejoice fully in both halves of our one being, in ourselves and in each other, never to be divided again from a complete union of the one with the other. He will be the cementing cause of our union, who is now that of this little separation. You will be present to me, and keep me ever present with you. I salute all my children, asking them to pray for me."

The Abbey of Dunes flourished under the care of its new Abbot. This was owing not only to the care of Robert, but because in all matters of doubt he had recourse to his Master at Clairvaulx. There had come to his Monastery one, who, during the time of probation, had shown himself by no means faithful, for which cause the Brethren had decreed to cast him out.

Robert however was, from his tender anxiety and fatherly care, unwilling to do so, without having first consulted his holy Father and Master, whose judgment on the matter appears in the following letter.

" Concerning the Brother you mention, who is not only unprofitable but even burdensome, apart from what yet lies hidden within, I give you the same counsel I would use myself. It appears to me from what you have related of him, that he has shown himself neither a likely subject, nor one who should be received. You may, therefore, reasonably and with a safe conscience, take away the evil one from among you, as he deserves. If, however, in your goodness, you are pleased to exalt mercy over judgment, you can still retain him with you without profession, as long as it seems well to you. I by all means advise you not to admit him to profession in his present state, but let him be again proved, if he may perhaps show himself such an one as he ought to be, and if not, the pruning knife must be used to cut him off,—lest one diseased sheep infect the whole flock."

Some time after Robert had been sent to Dunes in Flanders, it pleased the holy Father Bernard to visit him, at which time he preached a sermon to the Canons of S. Walburga, at Furnes, and staying awhile in the Monastery at Dunes, offered the holy sacrifice in the chapel of the blessed Martyr Lawrence. This chapel was therefore greatly venerated afterwards by the people, but now lies buried in the sand, having been thrown down to the ground by the madness of heretics.

Now when the happy and serene day arrived, on which the Blessed Father Bernard was to depart from this corruptible life to the better country, his sons, anguished with fear and distress, besought of him that he would name to them beforehand him whom he would wish to succeed him in the charge of the flock. He, consenting to their desire, chose and named Robert of Dunes to be their future Abbot.

This, indeed, had been revealed to one of the Brethren of Clairvaulx six or seven years before. For whilst two of them were conversing of the happy actions of their beloved Abbot, "Know you," said one of them, "how long our most Blessed Father will live?" He replying that he knew not, the other rejoined, "I know that he will abide six or seven years in the flesh, and then Robert of Dunes will be made Abbot of Clairvaulx."

How he knew this he did not then say, and he died before what he said was fulfilled. The mention of six or seven years seems to have been made, because six years were fully complete, but the seventh had not run through before the accomplishment of his prophecy.

Robert then at the very earnest entreaty of the Brethren of Clairvaulx, Bishops even and Abbots coming kneeling at his feet to persuade him, undertook the burden of his new charge. With great humility he fulfilled his pastoral duties, knowing, that even with the most eminent virtues, he could never bear comparison with the Saint who had preceded him.

Whilst he was Abbot a certain Monk of most holy conversation, and one who was highly esteemed amongst the Brethren was rapt into an extacy, and saw a glorious vision, which the Lord was pleased to show him for the consolation of His family at Clairvaulx. On the Tuesday following Easter, when he was paying his nightly praises with the rest in Choir, the hand of the Lord was upon him. And behold, opposite the middle of the Choir, high in the air, there appeared to him a

right hand, refulgent and glorious, which blessed
the assembled family as they praised His name
with psalms and hymns and spiritual canticles,
signing them solemnly once and again with the
lifegiving sign of the cross. The Spirit meanwhile spoke within his heart, saying, "This is
the Arm of the Lord, this is the Right Hand of
the Almighty."

On that same day two persons, according to the
twofold blessing of the Almighty Hand, entered as
postulants for the Order in the Monastery of
Dunes. The first was Andrew, Archdeacon of the
Church of Verdunes, a man of high rank. He
had had no intention of entering the Order, but
only came to pass a few days in retirement and
prayer. But when, that he might ask for their
prayers, he entered the Chapter of the Brethren,
being moved to compunction by the religious
order of that holy multitude, and their, as it were,
angelical manner of life, by the visitation of God's
Holy Spirit, he was changed into another man.
Indeed, with such earnestness of zeal did he for-
sake the world, that neither to bid farewell to his
friends, nor to set the affairs of his house in
order, would he return even an hour to it. He
did not loose the ties which bound him, but rather
he broke them in his impatience, that with the
less delay he might cleave with all the love of
his heart to Christ the Lord.

The second who came with him was a cleric
named Geoffrey, of a more humble grade of life,

but perhaps not inferior to him in virtuous life and nobility of heart. Both of them persevering in the Order began a strenuous warfare.

The forementioned Andrew endured grievous temptations in the first newness of his conversion, but The Hand which had given the benediction preserved him unhurt in all things. The triumph of the Right Hand of the Most High was for this reason all the more glorious, in proportion as the vessel in which He showed His mighty operation was weak and frail. Nurtured in extreme softness and delicacy, it was with much difficulty Andrew began to unlearn his former way of life. The task of embracing so severe a life, unused as he had been to any hardship, appeared so exceedingly difficult that, like another Lot, coming out of Sodom, he thought it would be impossible for him to save his soul in the mountain, he therefore proposed to turn aside to some Order of a less strict observance. He oftentimes made known to his spiritual Father the Blessed Robert these thoughts of his heart, and by his wholesome admonitions he was kept from fulfilling his intentions. At length, however, one day quite overcome by the storm of temptation, and losing all courage, he declared to the Abbot plainly that he could not endure any longer. Then the Abbot obtained of him, by prayers and kind words, that he would at least do violence to himself, and have patience till the third day. Having scarcely been able to gain thus much of him, he, on entering the Chapter, besought of all the Brethren to make common prayers for this tempted soul. The venerable Father himself also failed not to turn to God with most earnest supplication, entreating the Lord that He would deign to preserve, in His mercy, that sheep which the Enemy was endeavouring to snatch out of the fold.

On that same day, when the Novice approached the table, he found that pease had been served round as the food of the Brethren. It was a kind of food for which he felt the greatest loathing, more than for any other sort of vegetable. The taste of them was so nauseous to him, as sometimes to make him feel ready to be sick. He looked at the dish with disgust, and felt much troubled. Hardly could the persuasion of hunger induce his reluctant stomach to take a small quantity. When, oh! the goodness of God, how sweet and rich in mercy towards the tender and delicate, in order that in all the counsel of His Will may be accomplished, and His holy Name be glorified. For when the fore-mentioned Novice had scarce tasted the food set before him, he found in it a certain marvellous delicious savour, more delightful to the palate than that of either fish or flesh. With little delay he took his spoon, and made short work of the mess portioned out to him, even not resting till his dish was quite empty. But several times he fancied he could detect small pieces of fat in which he imagined the pease to have been stewed. And when dinner was over he, hastened to the Abbot to ask him if he had had any fat or dripping mixed with the food that day on his account. The Abbot said no. But, for his clearer conviction, the cook who prepared the dinner was sent for, who protested solemnly that no other thing had been used for the cooking but salt and water. When the Novice heard this, convinced of the truth, he saw plainly in it but a miracle of the Divine visitation in his regard, and, putting away all thoughts of leaving the Order, he gave great thanks to God for His mercy.

This miracle of God's grace was not given once or twice only, but for a long time afterwards he perceived in his food the same delicious savour; whence he learned by experience that God can do what He will, and that for the consolation of His servants He can give as delightful a savour to vegetables and legumes as to fish and flesh, so that he used often to remark, that fish and herbs were more delicious to him now than fatted meats and the dainties of the chase had been in former times.

The Blessed Robert had in his Monastery a certain Brother, Guicard by name, who ran the way leading to eternal life, without ever declining from it to the right hand or to the left. It pleased the Lord at length to put an end to the holy man's labours, that he might henceforth sleep and take his rest. When the hour drew near that he should be called out of the racecourse of this world, to receive the prize of his high calling in

14

heaven, the Reverend Abbot, with the rest of the
Brethren, were gone to rest on their beds. Then
a deep sleep from the Lord fell upon the Abbot,
and he beheld in a vision, and lo! two young men
of most beautiful aspect, whose countenance and
whose raiment shone white as the light, entering
into the choir of the Church of Clairvaulx, began
strewing over the pavement, as it were, lilies and
roses and violets, and various other kinds of
flowers in great abundance, so that the whole of
the floor seemed to be rendered beautiful by their
varied colours. The Abbot, however, astonished
at the sight, and, as it were, full of zeal for the
simplicity of the Order, said to them, "My good
young men, why is it that, contrary to our custom,
you have thought fit to strew the pavement with
these flowers, and to introduce a novelty of this sort
into our Monastery?" They answered him, "Do
not wonder, nor molest us in the execution of our
office, because there is to be celebrated, in this
very Choir presently, a new festival of a certain
Saint, on account of whose solemnity the angels
rejoice, and a hymn is sung to the Lord in Sion."
Whilst they were yet speaking to him, his mind
ravished with admiration at what he heard and
saw, the sound of the tablet announcing the approaching death of one of the Brethren roused
him from sleep, and he was called to accomplish,
according to the dignity of his office, that festival
which he already in spirit knew was to be celebrated. Hastening, therefore, with the rest of the

Brethren to the dying man, he with great devotion made the commendation of his soul, believing with confident certainty that he was the new Saint for whose assumption into rest the holy angels were about to keep a new festival and day of gladness.

Happy, truly happy are they, O Lord, whom Thou hast chosen and taken to Thyself; who, through the ardour of their penance, burn away whilst here all the rust of sin, that when they pass away to that life in which the Lord shall wash off the filth of the daughters of Sion with the tremendous spirit of judgment and the spirit of burning, they may require no purgation, but, without any obstacle of sin, may attain at once to blessedness and rest.

Robert had been three years and a half fulfilling his office as Abbot of Clairvaulx, when having employed faithfully and prudently the talent committed to him, he was introduced into the joy of his Lord, joined in the blessedness of his predecessor, though not equalling him in merits. Walking on the Good Friday, with naked feet, the cold entered piercingly into his limbs, and on Holy Saturday he was seized with such a fever, that with much difficulty he was taken from his stall to the infirmary by the hands of the Brethren, and there, after a few days illness, persevering steadfastly in his holy profession, he slept in the Lord on the 28th day of April. The remains of his

body were placed in a monument constructed in
the wall of the cloister of Clairvaulx, near the door
of the Church, where also other worthy Monks
rest in the Lord.

LIFE OF THE BLESSED AIMON,

MONK OF SAVIGNI.

THE Blessed Aimon was born in the diocese of Avranche. Educated in polite letters, he became a very learned man. He was a man who feared God and eschewed the follies of a worldly life.

Having distributed all his goods to the poor, he retired to Savigni, at the time when that Abbey was first founded. He had a particular charity for lepers whilst yet in the world, and used to wash their feet, and render them every assistance. He was beloved not only by his Brethren, but also by persons in the world. There were certain individuals of high quality who used him as the physician of their souls, opening to him all their secrets, and taking his advice for the conduct of their life.

He was always in prayer, afflicting his body with rigorous abstinences, and preserving himself, as far as possible, from every idle and superfluous word. His sleep was short, and he was almost always reciting psalms. His Superiors having thought that he should be raised to the priesthood, he received with trembling the imposition of hands. This grace filled him so with the fulness

of the Spirit, that he was without ceasing penetrated with God. Often he forgot to eat, and his
food had no taste to him. He received from
heaven extraordinary graces when he offered the
holy Mysteries.

One day when he was offering the great Sacrifice, and profoundly inclined, was uttering the
words, "We suppliantly beseech Thee Almighty
God to command that this sacrifice may be carried
by Thy holy Angels," &c., he saw the altar all
surrounded with Angels clad in albs exceedingly
white, and with countenances full of reverential
joy. One there was, who in stature and in beauty
surpassed the others. This glorious one, taking
himself alone the Sacred Host from the altar,
raised it up on high, and presented it to the Divine
Majesty. All the other Angels who were present
united themselves to this one, and showed as
much reverence and as much joy as if they had
each themselves taken the Sacred Host, and presented it themselves to the Majesty of God. After
this vision was over the holy man found the
Sacred Host on the Altar after the accustomed
manner.

Another time, scarcely had he finished the words
of consecration, when he saw the heavens opened,
and Jesus Christ present before him, who, bowing
the head to him, came to him with an exceeding
great goodness, and immediately all the powers of
his soul were filled with an unspeakable heavenly
sweetness, penetrating to the inmost depths of his

heart. He heard then by a marvellous secret impression the words: "This is the Son of God who vouchsafes to appear for thy consolation."

This vision so ravished his senses, that his soul, without being separated from the body, was elevated to such a state as to have no sentiment of what was before him. His eyes saw nothing, neither the altar nor what was upon it, no nor anything whatsoever. God alone occupied all. That joy, unspeakable and glorious, with which he was filled, possessed him entirely, and, being united to God, no other object could for a moment turn the soul from Him. Returning to himself, he completed the holy sacrifice rather like an angel than a man.

God honoured him with various other gifts. He knew the secrets of the hearts, and he cured by his prayers desperate maladies. By his prayers he obtained the conversion of several great sinners, and God revealed to him the day of his death long before that day arrived. He had made known to him by revelation the glory of a certain Monk named Peter, who was united to him by a particular friendship. This Monk had such a care for the purity of his conscience, that he could not bear to see himself sullied by the slightest fault, without at once having recourse to the sacrament of penance. The Blessed Aimon he had chosen as the guide of his soul, and after his death as the holy man was praying by his grave he was ravished out of himself, and in his ecstasy he saw a great multitude of Saints shining with glory, among whom he recognized the Blessed Peter. Peter spoke to him, and told him that God had given him this glory as a recompense for the care he had taken to keep his conscience clean. The Blessed Aimon died full of days in the year of Redemption 1174.

LIFE OF BLESSED ALEXANDER,

MONK OF FOIGNI.

ALEXANDER came of the royal family of the kings of Scotland. He had three brothers and one sister, who all of them chose the poverty of the cross rather than the worldly greatness, which was theirs by birth. The first quitted wife and country; the second became a Hermit; the third resigned an Archbishopric to enter the Cistercian Order.

Alexander was the fourth. His father seeing that his other sons had entered all of them on a Religious course, wished at least to retain this one in the world to succeed to his crown. The young Prince was yet but sixteen years of age. His sister Matilda, at that time twenty years of age, seeing that her father was bent upon engaging her young brother in the world, took him aside one day and said to him, " What do you think to do, my brother ? Your elder brothers have renounced the world, and their country, to obtain heaven. They have despised an earthly kingdom to secure a heavenly. There remains but you to succeed to the kingdom, but consider how this earthly crown may make you lose that which is heavenly and eternal."

These words had such an effect on the young Prince, that, melting into tears, he said to his sister, " What must I do ? Do you counsel me. I am willing to do whatever you bid me." Matilda, full of joy, made known her plans to her brother, of quitting her country and going into France. Without making known to any one their design, they changed each their dress for common clothing, and, leaving the palace, made their way to the coast by the guidance of God, and crossed over into France, where they took the road to Picardy, and being arrived at Foigni, a Cistercian Abbey, in the Diocese of Laon, Alexander demanded the habit of a Convert Brother, and was sent to pasture the cows, and also to make cheese and butter, which his sister had already taught him to do.

Matilda then took leave of her brother, telling him she should never see him again in this life. This separation cost the young Prince more than all the rest that he had given up. Matilda withdrew to a place ten or twelve miles from Foigni, where she lived in a hovel supporting herself by her labour. In the time of harvest she gleaned after the reapers. Her prayers were so long that her knees became quite hard. She paid such attention to prayer, that she was unconscious of the sound of thunder, and saw not the lightning.

Matilda and Alexander were so faithful to their resolution never to see one another, that they never enquired after one another. No one of that part knew that they were brother and sister. Yet

often they were very near each other, without
knowing it, because Alexander had to take his
cows to pasture sometimes a very short distance
from the cottage where his sister lived. They
kept strictly also the secret of their high birth.
Still there was something about the manners of
Alexander, which made some suspect he was of
noble parentage. At last, shortly before his death,
his Superior obliged him under obedience to say
who he was.

It happened also that one day when a great lord
of that country was pursuing a wild boar, the
animal turned round to defend itself. Having
dismounted and seized his weapons, he was taken
on a sudden with great fear. Alexander, who was
pasturing his cows close by, seeing how matters
stood, approached, and taking the arms from his
hands, attacked the boar and killed it instantly.
The lord was not a little surprized at the daring
hardihood of this action, and at his address in
the use of these weapons; and falling on his neck,
said, "I do not know who you are, but I know
very well that you have had another occupation
than that which you now follow."

Alexander, having now finished the task allotted
to him by God in his hidden life, went to receive
the reward of his labours on the fourth day of May,
A.D. 1229.

Whilst a Monk was one day praying at his
grave, the Blessed Alexander appeared to him,
brighter than the sun, and having two crowns, one

on his head and the other in his hands. The
Brother asked him how it was he had two crowns.
The Blessed Alexander answered that God had
given him one instead of the earthly crown he had
for His sake renounced, and the other for the
labours he had undergone. He then added that
for a surety of the truth of this, the Brother should
be at once delivered from his infirmities, which
accordingly happened.

As for Matilda, being recognized by some persons who came from Scotland, she wished much to
fly, but was hindered by the inhabitants of the
country, and ending her life there, many miracles
were accorded to her sanctity after her death.

LIFE OF SAINT PETER,

ARCHBISHOP OF TARENTAISE.

SAINT PETER of Tarentaise was born in the year of our Lord 1101. His parents had a small farm in the diocese of Vienne, which they themselves cultivated. They passed their lives in great simplicity, giving large alms to the poor, and hospitable towards Religious men.

At that time the Order of Citeaux, like a fruitful vine, was everywhere shooting forth its branches. Not far from their place of abode Pope Callixtus had planted the Monastery of Bonnevaux. Peter's parents became great friends of the Abbot John, a man of great holiness of life.

Their eldest son, Lambert, was brought up from childhood in learned studies. Peter, the second, had other occupations assigned to him, but so eager was he for learning, that he advanced rapidly with scarce any teaching, by a sort of divine unction, to the great marvel of all who beheld him.

In one year he learned the whole Psalter of David by heart. The Lord prevented him with the blessings of sweetness, so that even in his tender years he was a lover of grave books, and took no delight in boyish games.

At that time the mother of Peter having ceased

bearing children, his parents, by mutual agreement, lived henceforth as brother and sister, in
holy chastity, that thus, as far as it was possible
in the world, they might practise the perfection of
the Religious life.   They gave their best beds to
the use of the poor and of pilgrims, of whom their
house became the hospital, whilst they themselves
slept upon straw.   They sought to relieve the
wants of the Monks, especially of the Carthusians
and those of Bonnevaux, bringing them provisions
and receiving in exchange spiritual doctrine.   The
father of Peter wore a rough hair-shirt next his
skin.   Nor would they receive any Church benefices for their children who were of the Clergy, a
thing which the most pious parents were in the
habit of doing.   Peter, by the advice of Abbot
John, joined the Monks of Bonnevaux in A.D.
1118.   Lambert, his brother, was drawn by his
example to embrace the Monastic life at Casiriac,
of which house he afterwards became the Abbot.

Peter, after having filled various offices in the
Abbey of Bonnevaux, was elected Abbot of the
Monastery of Stamedium, a new Monastery founded
by Abbot John, A.D. 1128.   It was called Stamedium as standing middle where two Counties meet
together.   Who can recount how kind he was to
the wayfarers and the poor, giving them, to the
best of his power, food and clothing, whilst he
himself was ill clad, and had for his meat but
bread and water, with a few herbs, having no seasoning, unless perhaps a little salt.   If he went

on a journey he took care to carry with him some
loaves and cheeses for the poor whom he might
meet with, and he always took his repast, if possible, on the road side, that his table might be open
to the traveller. The poorer a man was the more
welcome at his board. Prince Amedee of Savoy
much esteemed the holy man, and conferred on
the Monastery among other things a vineyard in
Mount Meliorac, with buildings for store-houses.

In A.D. 1138 Peter was chosen Bishop of Tarentaise ; he would not, however, consent to the election. But the General Chapter commanded him
to accept, and thus constrained by the authority of
the Fathers and especially of S. Bernard himself,
he dared no longer refuse. His manner of life
was however little changed from what it had been
before. His dress was poor, his table spare, his
sleep scanty. If better clothes were brought him
they did not make a long stay, for he gave them
to some one else. When he went to the Roman
court, he always would have the poor satisfied,
before he began his own dinner, so that it sometimes happened that the whole of what had been
prepared was given away. The holy man being
delighted at such a thing falling out, so that he
might be left to shift without any regular dinner.

He was exceedingly diligent in his diocese, com-
pensating for labours of the hands by continual
journeyings. He could no longer observe silence.
He did not, however, allow to his tongue subtilties

of words or human eloquence, but only such words
as were simple and fit to edify the hearers.

When the new Bishop came into residence,
he found to his great grief that the Service of God
was negligently carried through in such a manner
as not only not to deserve a reward, but rather to
merit a curse. The houses of the Bishop and of
the Clergy were falling into ruins. The tithes of
the diocese were in the hands often of laymen, men
of power,—the lives of the priests far from praise-
worthy. Relying upon prayer rather than on his
own industry, he began to set on foot a new course
of things. He removed the secular clergy of his
Cathedral, men of high family, and instead of
them brought in Regular Canons, himself coming
to the Choir, and living in the Cloister, so that
they might become under his eye a pattern to both
Clergy and laymen. He also took the tithes out
of the hands of the great men, employing sometimes the censures of the Church, and sometimes
redeeming them with money. He took care that
no Church in his diocese should be without suitable things for Divine worship, books, palls, and
vestments. To provide for each a silver chalice,
he ordained that eggs should be gathered from
house to house, where the place was poor, and
sold each week till the necessary sum was procured. He took care also that all the Clergy
should have a decent house where they might live,
not in luxury but in moderate comfort. The
Churches also, where it was necessary, he repaired

and adorned. His own house at all times kept open hospitality for strangers, but it was especially thronged for the three months before the harvest, when the poor feel the greatest want. He provided for the wants of the poor, indeed, in all places of his diocese, and his tears would fall in compassion, when cases of affliction were brought before him.

Once meeting an old woman shivering with the cold of an Alpine winter, and but half clad, "Alas!" he cried, "there is my mother perishing with cold." Then turning aside out of the pathway, he stripped off his robe from beneath his Cowl, and returning after awhile presented it to the woman. He was observed by his attendants to be pale and trembling, but it was only when they had reached home that they discovered the cause, and they were obliged to put the Bishop into a warm bed till he should recover from the effects of his holy imprudence.

The venerable Bishop worked many miracles wherever he went, so that continually the blind received their sight, the lame were enabled to walk, and the dumb to speak through his blessing. But desiring to remain hidden, he referred the cures to the merits of other Saints.

It chanced one day when three men were in prison, and in chains, the keepers were playing at dice before the doors, when suddenly the holy Bishop, being invoked, appeared. Their chains were loosed, and opening the door he led them

15

forth through the very midst of the guards into a place of safety, the guards appearing not to observe them at all.

The place where he was wont to preach to the crowds was far from any town, so that provisions had to be brought from a distance. One Sunday, on which day several thousands were present, there was scarce anything in the house, the weather having been so tempestuous, that no provisions had been brought. The man of God, however, bade that the usual Sunday meal should be served to the crowd. In vain it was told him that it was impossible. He commanded that what they had in the house should be cooked, and served out to the multitudes. The hall was filled with a crowd, and after they had been satisfied, others were brought in, till the whole had eaten enough, and yet there was still found abundance over after that all had been filled.

The man of God was struck with a holy fear at the glory these great signs brought upon him. "Ah!" said he to himself, "what doest thou? What will it profit thee if thou gain the whole world, and lose thy own soul? O glory, glory! Thou deceivest those whom thou callest happy. Thou bringest low those whom thou exaltest." With such thoughts he determined with himself to flee from the danger that hung over him.

In the silence of the night, he left the house with a single companion, whom he sent back after a short while, having met with a man who might

serve him as a guide. He then, changing his
guide several times so as to escape discovery, made
his journey through bye-ways, till he reached a
Monastery of the Cistercian Order in Germany.
Here, being wholly unknown, and not able to
speak the language of that country, he remained
like one deaf and dumb, going in and out as a
simple Monk. How great was his joy. He kept
sabbath now to God according to the desire of his
heart, and was well pleased with his sabbath rest.

In the morning his whole household was in
amazement as to what had become of him. They
sought for him in his chamber, they sought him in
the streets and broadways of the city, and found
him not. There is no one to tell how he is gone
down into his garden of aromatical spices to feed
on spiritual delights and gather lilies. The report
goes forth among the people that their pastor is
fled. The light of their eyes is gone from them,
and their glad feasts are turned into mourning.
A search is made through all that country, but in
vain.

A certain young man, however, who from a
child had been brought up with him, went into
Germany, God so ordering it, and came to the
Monastery, in which the holy old man was hidden.
As the Brethren went out to labour in the morning, this young man diligently marked the face of
each, when to his joy he saw amongst the rest
that of the man he sought. At once he knew

him, and falling down before him, caught him by the feet and would not let him go.

All were in astonishment at this sight, but when they knew who it was, they also in turn knelt before him, being sorry for the little reverence with which they had treated him, and complaining because he had hid his light under a bushel. They all wept till he exceeded, lamenting that from his thirsty lips the sweet cup of wisdom was thus rudely snatched away. And who can tell with what joy he was received back again by his own, as it were one alive from the dead, for it went about in all that land that a prophet had arisen mighty in word and work.

Before the holy man was made Abbot, he took both his parents out of the wicked world, placing his father in Bonnevaux and his mother in a Cistercian Convent of Nuns at S. Paul's. His younger brother Andrew also, he placed at Bonnevaux.

Both his father and mother died in a good old age, and were buried by their son Peter with tender piety. In those days Victor III. engaged the Church in a great schism, the Emperor Frederic thrusting him forward, and using violence against all who opposed him. The holy Archbishop, not regarding the person of men, set himself against the Emperor, defending the cause of the just. Notwithstanding this, the Emperor, whilst he drove into exile other Bishops and Abbots, honoured him with great reverence. " What doest thou, O Emperor ?" said a wicked man, Herbert, a Bishop in the schism. "This man declareth us heretics and giveth us to anathema, and thou honourest him like an angel of the Lord." The Emperor replied to him, "If I show myself contrary to men, wouldst thou have me also evidently to fight against God ?"

Alexander III. sent for the holy man to Rome, and he went through Italy confirming the Catholics, as he had already done in Burgundy and Lorraine. His name alone drew many to the cause of the Catholic Pope.

In A.D. 1174, he went to the Monastery of Louguet at the request of the Bishop of Langres, to dedicate a new altar in memory of S. Bernard. A certain wretch among the crowd who were present stole a small cross containing a particle of the wood, on which had died the Saviour of the world. One of the Brethren told the Archbishop. The holy man publicly pronounced upon the robber a grievous curse, commanding him in the name of Christ not to leave the Monastery till he had restored the cross. The man endeavoured to get away, but could not do so, though he persisted in his evil design till after the Archbishop was gone. He could, however, in no wise leave the place, being withheld by an invisible force, till he had restored the cross to the altar from which he had stolen it. A person also who had stolen a Cowl could not get away with his booty from the precincts of the Monastery, and at last, coming to the porter, threw it down at his feet, saying, "Take your cloak, which I have several times tried to carry away with me, but have not been able."

The Archbishop received an order from the Pope to go into France to try and reconcile the King of England and the King of the French. On his road he stopped at Pruilli, a Cistercian Abbey in the diocese of Sens. As all the provisions they had were not enough for the crowds who followed him, the holy man bade them be of good courage and give freely, for God would bless their store. They believed his word and gave to the multitudes, and by God's blessing a few loaves went further than at other times a great quantity of bread.

There lived, not far from the Abbey, a soldier, whose son was blind. This man took his boy, hoping to have him healed by the Archbishop's prayers, for he had heard of the wonders done by his hands. Whilst he was coming, he was met by certain, bringing blessed bread from the Abbey. He begged a small quantity with which he made a salve, and put it to the eyes of the boy, and he immediately received his sight.

King Louis sent certain gentlemen of his court to meet the Archbishop as soon as he heard of his coming. A great many miracles, too many to recount, were wrought by him as he passed along. The two Kings with a great multitude of people were gathered together at a town on the borders

of Normandy, called Chaumont. The King of
England on his arrival flew to meet him, and
when he saw him yet a great way off, he descended
quickly from his horse, and ran and threw himself
at his feet embracing them. The Cowl of the
holy Archbishop had suffered much from the devotion of the people, who, to obtain a relic from his
person, had cut away much of the lower portion.
The King, however, not content with a fragment,
would have the whole. He endeavoured therefore
to draw it off. It was in vain the Archbishop
became indignant, and threatened even to lay the
King under a curse. The King was bent on having the Cowl, and did not desist till he had got
the possession of it. When the Brethren who
came with the Archbishop asked him complain-
ingly what use an old Cowl was among his royal
treasures, he replied, " If only you knew the marvels that have been wrought by this man's girdle,
which some years ago I procured, you would not
speak in this fashion."

Whilst the Archbishop stayed here treating
with the principal persons of the conditions of
peace, there came a poor widow with her daughter, a child born dumb. She, thinking her un-
fortunate lot and that of her daughter of more
moment than the enmities of kings, or the peril of
whole countries, thrust herself forward, some for-
bidding her, and others murmuring. The Archbishop did not despise her, but listening to her
humble petition, moistened his thumb with spittle

from his mouth, and with it made upon the lips of the dumb child the sign of the cross. He then made her speak a few words, himself first uttering them to her, and so restored her perfectly healed to her mother.

Another day, whilst treating of affairs with the two Kings and the Count of Flanders, a mother came with her son, now twelve years of age, who had been blind from his seventh year. The holy man, seeing that she was unable to approach him, being kept back by the servants of the Kings, ordered her to be brought forward with her son. He then learned from her the cause of her distress, and taking the boy to him caressingly, with his hand upon his hair, he asked of him what he wished. Upon which the boy answered, "My Lord, that I may see." The Archbishop taking a piece of money put it into his hand. Then moistening his fingers with spittle from his mouth, he signed the eyes of the boy and the top of his head with the sign of the cross, at the same time pausing awhile in prayer. Now the Kings were looking on in great wonder, doubting indeed if the holy man were in earnest, or were really doing anything, when of a sudden the boy in a transport of joy uttered a cry, and said, "Oh! mother, I see everything. I see trees, and men, and all things that are round me." At these words the mother, raising her hands and her eyes to heaven, knelt down before the man of God giving him thanks. The King of the French also seeing so evident a miracle, of whose truth he had diligently enquired, knelt down also to adore the divine power present in this gift of healing. He kissed the head of the boy and his eyes so lately opened, and put money into his hand. Many others followed so great an example.

The Ash Wednesday of the year 1161 having arrived, the Archbishop gave the Ashes in the Monastery of Mortimer to the King of England and all who were with him.

A certain soldier, who had lost the sight of one eye by a wound from a javelin, begged to be healed with much instancy of prayer. The man of God, however, excused himself, saying, that the work was beyond his strength, but as the man persisted, he touched his eyes, telling him that, if he would wait for it, he should receive the mercy of God, and presently his sight was restored to him, like that of the other eye.

The much longed-for peace was concluded between the two Kings in the month of May that same year.

Having now fulfilled for three-and-thirty years the office of Bishop, it pleased the Lord to translate His servant to a better world. As he approached the Abbey of Bellevaux, he was taken with a fever. His sickness, however, did not lessen the cheerfulness and kindness with which he performed all that was asked of him, though little able for the task. It was on the Feast of the Finding of the Holy Cross that he passed away, fortified with the sacraments of the Lord, his children singing and praying around him. Thus he was gathered to his fathers. Three days and nights watch was kept round his sacred body with psalms and holy canticles, and then the Archbishop of Besançon laid his body in a tomb before the Altar of the ever Virgin Mary. He was seventy-three years old at his death, in A.D. 1174. Twenty years before he became a Monk; ten years at Bonnevaux, ten years at Stamedium, and thirty-three as Archbishop make up his course. His Feast is kept on the ninth of May by order of Pope Celestin III. His translation was made in A.D. 1192, on the eleventh of September.

OF THE BLESSED EUSTACE,

ABBOT OF HEMMENRODE.

THE Blessed Eustace was in his youth brought up in all learning, and wisdom of letters. The fame of his singular virtue, when he became a Monk at Hemmenrode, went through all Germany, and at the death of the Abbot he was chosen by the lots of the Brethren. He greatly loved the intimacy of holy persons, consecrated to God. The Most High made his virtues known not only to those within his Monastery, but he was venerated as a Saint also by those without.

On the Feast of the Assumption of the most Blessed Mary, a certain Virgin, named Christina, of the Cistercian Order, standing in her choir, was rapt into an ecstasy of mind. She saw before her the Abbot Eustace, who was on a visit at the Abbey of Heisterbach. The holy Abbot, after finishing the gospel, had begun the hymn "*Te Deum,*" when the heavens were opened immediately above the assembled Community, and she saw the walls of the Oratory, which were then of wood, as if they had been of purest gold on each side. Above appeared the glorious Mary Mother of God, seated on a throne, and round her a multitude of Saints, who appeared all young, as it were of the age of five-and-twenty years. When the Choir of Monks sang "*Sanctus, Sanctus, Sanctus*," the most Blessed Virgin, manifesting her joy at their devotion, let down over them, by a golden chain, a crown of wonderful beauty, such as are used to be hung in Churches. In place of the knott, there was a jewel exceedingly precious, and all sparkling, in which was written, "O clement, O pious, O sweet Virgin Mary." From the jewel came forth three arms, which held the crown hanging from them. From the name "Mary" came forth rays of light. These rays lit up the names of the Monks then in Choir, which were all written round about the crown. According to the merits of each Monk, so was the brightness of the letters, with which his name was written, and the position in which it found place. In these things there was a great diversity, and the names of some newly converted shone far more brightly, and were in a higher position than the names of some, who had laboured long in the Monastic life. For it seems that not the space of time, or the labour of body, is considered with the Lord, but the fervour of spirit in His servants. When the Choir came to the words, "*In te, Domine, speravi: non confundar in æternum*," the crown was drawn up by her into heaven, as she uttered these words, "As I am now in glory, so shall these be with me for everlasting."

LIFE OF SAINT ASCELINE,

CISTERCIAN NUN.

A SCELINE was a near kinswoman of the most
holy Father Bernard. She was born in the
year of Redemption 1121. Her father's name was
Joubert, a man noble, and of high virtue. Her
mother was great in her charity towards the poor.
They lived in a small village not far from Clairvaulx.

Whilst the infant Asceline was yet in the womb
this pious mother made many prayers for her
future offspring. She received a revelation from
the Most High that her child should be exceedingly dear in His sight, and that the grace of God
should be with her.

About five years after the birth of the child, the
father of Asceline died, and her mother, desiring
to belong now entirely to God, retired with the
young child to a nunnery near to Boulancour, in
the diocese of Troy. She placed herself and her
child under the guidance of the most holy Father
Bernard. The little Asceline, though she showed
great love of holy things, yet was not free from
the faults of childhood, and sometimes she used
to steal little things to eat, or to play with. God
did not leave her without reproof in these things,

but she felt as it were some one pulling her by her dress, and at the same time she heard a voice saying, " Why do you do that ? Never do such a thing again." Although this voice sounded clearly in her ears, there was no human creature near her to utter it. Knowing, therefore, that it must come from God, she thanked Him much for His kind care in thus drawing her out of the meshes of iniquity.

When she was twelve years old she conceived a great dislike for all the things of the world, and separated herself as far as she could from all earthly occupations, applying her whole soul to prayer. At this time she began to have visions sometimes of the spirits of the Blessed.

Now it came to pass that, not being yet a Nun, she went out of the Monastery to a place where she might assist in making wax tapers for the altar, a young man saw her, and getting an opportunity of speaking with her alone, asked whether she could not love him. This sweet young maiden, knowing nothing, said that indeed she would love him, if he would renounce the world and become a Monk. The young man consented to do so out of mere deceit, and entered the house of the Canons Regular at Boulancour. He contrived to send verses of his own composition to the young Asceline, who suspected no evil. But one day, when in her own Convent, there stood suddenly before her a leprous man, who said to her, " Beware, my child ; that bad man, whom you trust, is a messenger of Satan to destroy you." The leper disappeared, and could nowhere be found. She told all this to her mother, who returned thanks to God with her for this warning. As for the wretched man, finding his wiles discovered, he returned back again into the world, and gave himself up to a wicked life. Asceline was more cautious of herself for the future.

After this, Asceline and her mother obtained permission of their superiors to retire into a desert not far from the Monastery. Here the Blessed Asceline cut off her hair with her own hands, not desiring to have her beauty seen by mortal eyes, but only desiring to be beautiful in the eyes of the heavenly Bridegroom.

Now it happened one day, when she went with her Mother to the Chapel to receive instructions from the Priest, their Director, they found the door fast. Then the Blessed Asceline, kneeling down by an impulse of the Holy Ghost, besought the Lord to give her a sign that He would preserve her amongst His pure Virgins by opening the door of the Chapel. She had no sooner finished the words of her prayer, than the door of the Chapel opened of itself, and they both entered, the Blessed Asceline giving thanks to God for this fresh token of His love.

She was not, however, without temptations against that holy chastity, which she loved so much. In order to overcome them she exercised herself in the most menial services. She also gave herself a severe discipline seven times a day, making frequent prostrations before the Divine Majesty. She lacerated her body with thorns and briars, rubbing her face with ashes to disfigure its beauty. At this time she was but fourteen years of age. One day, when she was praying the Lord with tears, that He would give her a place in the company of Virgins, S. John the Evangelist appeared to her, and said, "Be constant, my daughter, and you shall surely have a crown among the Virgins of Jesus Christ."

Although the Blessed Asceline was still young, yet her holiness of life was such that the Nuns chose her as their Prioress. But in the year of grace 1149, the Canons of Boulancour, having embraced the Cistercian Rule, these Nuns were obliged to leave, and, by the advice of the most holy Father Bernard, the Prioress Asceline, entered a Convent of Benedictine Nuns at Polengey, where his own niece was Abbess. She was now twenty-eight years of age, and being made Sacristan, she gave herself more than ever to prayer with an abundance of tears. One day, as she was thus weeping at prayer, she heard a voice, saying, "Tears that come from the heart are a second Baptism, if he who weeps over his faults does not return to them."

Besides the Divine Office the Blessed Asceline used to recite a whole psalter privately every day. On Saturdays and all Feasts of the most holy Virgin, she said a thousand Ave Marias. She added also two hundred prostrations to demand pardon of God for her offences, and took the discipline whilst·she recited thirty psalms. The grace she desired to be most thankful for was the continual thought of the presence of God, which accompanied her at all times.

One day, one of the daughters of the King of France came to see her in the season of Advent, but the Blessed Asceline not willing to break the silence or break off from her prayers, the princess returned without seeing her, not desiring to press upon her. None of these austerities, which she practised, were undertaken without the permission of the Abbess.

Having remained four years at Polengey, the Blessed Asceline returned to her old Monastery near to that of Boulancour, which was now a Cistercian Abbey. Here she delivered some persons from demoniacal possession by the touch of her veil. A woman in the diocese of Cologne had been tormented by the devil for fifteen years. The devil who possessed her declared he would not depart from her, unless driven out by the Nun Asceline, of the Monastery near Boulancour. The Archbishop therefore sent, begging her to come. She did so, and the woman was delivered from her tormentor. The Archbishop offered the Blessed Asceline jewels and gold, as tokens of gratitude, but she begged instead some relics of S. Ursula.

The Almighty God honoured Asceline by vari-

16

ous revelations. The Steward of a Cistercian Abbey, tempted by avarice, had passed a fraud on a widow. In punishment of this.God caused the whole of the wine of the Monastery to be spoiled. The Abbot, judging that this was not an accident, besought the Mother Asceline to ask of God why it was that this had fallen out. God revealed the fault of the Steward, which He punished also by another chastisement. A soldier set fire to the granaries, and almost all the provision of corn was consumed.

When the great Father Bernard passed from this world, he appeared at that moment to the Mother Asceline, ascending to heaven in the appearance of a dove. Her own time of departure at last came. She called her Nuns around her, exhorting them to despise the world, and to be faithful to their Spouse. She gave up her spirit in great peace in the year of grace 1195, on Friday, after Pentecost, being then seventy-four years of age. Miracles were wrought by her relics after her death, and she was buried in the same tomb with the Blessed Gozevin, Monk of that house, and of Blessed Hemeline. Her name occurs in the Cistercian Menology on the eighteenth of May.

LIFE OF BLESSED GILBERT,

ABBOT OF SWINSHED.

THE Blessed Gilbert of Hoyland was from his youth given to the pursuit of the things of God, increasing in knowledge and grace as he grew in years. He gave himself to the study of theology, in which he made much profit, and was learned in the holy Scriptures. Retiring to Clairvaulx he drank deep of the spirit of the most holy Father Bernard, fashioning his mind and soul after the model of this great example. In A.D. 1163 he was chosen Abbot of the Monastery of Swinshed in the diocese of Lincoln, in England. In the government of his Monks he was full of goodness and humility, sweet and affable in his manner, and upright in speech. Such discipline had he that he seemed to have no passions of anger or impatience or other unseemly thing. He had the consolation to see his Brethren walking before the Lord in all holiness and righteousness of a good conversation, loving God and full of good works.

The holy Abbot, besides his Monastery, had under his guidance a Convent of Nuns who lived in greatest sanctity. There was in this Convent a Nun whose holiness of conversation was such that

she had banished from her heart all the affections
of flesh and blood, all care for the things of the
body, and in general everything that could in any
way disquiet her heart or remove her thoughts
ever so little from the contemplation of those heavenly exercises, which were the only objects of her
burning desires. One day, when she was at prayer,
she felt her heart penetrated with such a wonderful sweetness, that it destroyed all affection for
created things, silenced all the movements of the
mind, and fixed its gaze upon heaven, in such a
manner, that immediately, as it were bidding
adieu to all earthly things, it could not restrain its
flight towards God. But lifted up above herself,
she found herself surrounded with a glorious and
incomprehensible light, and saw nothing but the
sovereign Being, who is the principle of all that
exists.

This light was not common light, nor, like a
body, had it any extension of length or breadth,
nevertheless, in a wonderful manner, it enclosed
her on all sides in such a way as cannot be expressed.

This blessed soul, being in this light, remained
a long hour ravished in God, till the Sisters came
and with great difficulty brought her out of this
ravishment back to her bodily senses. Now after
this time the like thing happened often to her.
The other Nuns beholding it, desired to know how
such a thing happened to her, that she was ravished out of herself; and, willing to have a share

of the same grace, several began after her example
to renounce all care, and all disquietudes, concerning the things of this life, giving themselves
without ceasing to prayer and tears.

The Almighty God was pleased to regard fa-
vourably the simplicity and uprightness of their
hearts, and heard their desires. They also began
to experience in themselves that happiness, which
up till now they had only admired in another, and
sometimes, even against their own will, they found
themselves surrounded with this wonderful light,
when in the midst of their Sisters.

There was one, however, a Nun of very great
discretion, who knowing that one must not believe
every spirit, attributed what happened to the Sisters to some fantastic illusion, or some strange
malady, and thought that in no way ought they to
make any consideration of all these visions. One
day this Nun said to one of those who were favoured with this grace, "How is it that nothing
of this kind ever happens to me?" The Sister
answered, "It is because you have no faith in
what we tell you, and that you love not in others
a gift which you have not yourself." The incredulous Nun then asked the Sister to pray for
her to God, that, if these visions came from Him
He would be pleased to favour her with them.
They both of them then betook themselves to
prayer, but without any result. The incredulous
Nun then complained to the other that she did not
receive the promised grace. She received for

answer that she must first renounce all affection
to the things of this world, and be occupied only
with the thought of God. The other then demanded whether she ought not to pray for her
friends and benefactors, received this answer:
" When you aim at elevating yourself to heavenly
things by contemplation, you must remit into the
hands of God those whom you love, as if you were
about to die, bidding adieu to all creatures, and
sighing after the possession of Him, who must be
the only object of your love."

The Nun, hardly crediting these words, again
begged the Sister to obtain for her from God the
grace of experiencing this kind of visions, if they
indeed come from Him. She added, however,
" Yet I do not desire that my soul may be so ravished or taken out of my body, as that I should
have no memory of anything, especially of my
friends. I ask for nothing, but to know if this
thing really is of God."

The gracious Lord, who knew the purity and
uprightness of her heart, was pleased to vouchsafe
to her, as she had desired. On a certain Good
Friday, as she was pondering in her mind over
this matter, she found herself on a sudden surrounded with the Divine Light, and was ravished
out of herself, and lifted up to the contemplation
of heavenly things, in a most unspeakable manner.
Unable to endure this incomprehensible light, she
demanded to be recalled to the view of the Passion
of Jesus Christ, and in a moment she saw in the

spirit Jesus Christ fastened to the cross, pierced with the nails, His Side opened by the lance, and His Blood flowing forth from feet and hands, and He Himself gazing on her with such a sweet kind look. Then she burst into tears, and coming back to herself she now gave credence to her Sisters, but did not think herself strong enough to endure that Light, so bright and glorious, which ravished her out of herself to such an elevated contemplation.

This relation the holy Abbot Aelred makes of the Nuns under the guidance of the Blessed Gilbert. So esteemed was Gilbert in the Order, that being considered by his Superiors to be filled with the spirit of the great Father Bernard, now loosed from the workshop of the body, they commanded him to continue the explication of Solomon's Canticle of Canticles. Gilbert unwillingly did what he thought himself unworthy to do, forced by the weight of their authority. Death however surprised him in the midst of his task, after completing forty-eight beautiful sermons, having so much the style of the most holy Father Bernard, that they might to his honour have been supposed to be his work.

He went to his rest about the year of grace 1166.

LIFE OF BLESSED HENRY,

ARCHBISHOP OF RHEIMS.

HENRY, brother of King Louis of France, brought up in the royal court, was yet converted as it were by a miracle, to the poverty of the Cistercian Rule. He had come to speak to Bernard, the man of God, on a matter of worldly business, and when visiting the Convent commended himself piously to the prayers of the Brethren. The holy Father in answer, said, "I have confidence in the Lord, that you will not end your life as you now are, but that very presently you will prove by your proper experience the efficacy of those prayers which you have asked for."

On that very day was this word fulfilled to the astonishment of many, the whole Community being filled with joy at the conversion of such a youth. His companions however, and his whole retinue, received the tidings, as if they had seen his dead corpse carried out, with loud lamentations. One especially, named Andrew of Paris, spared neither insults nor blasphemies, calling out that Henry was drunk and mad. Henry, however, on his part, prayed the man of God in particular for the conversion of this man. The holy man in the hearing of many, said, "Let him be. His soul is in bitterness : nevertheless do not be troubled concerning him, for he is yours." And when Henry, conceiving hope, urged him to speak to Andrew, the man of God with a rather severe look, said, " What is this you say ? Did I not tell you he is yours ?" Now Andrew heard this, for he was himself standing by, and he thought within himself, as he afterwards confessed, " By this I know you are a false prophet, for I am certain that you have now spoken a word, which will never come to pass. I shall take care publicly to reproach you with this before the King and the court, that your falsity may be known by all."

But how much to be admired is God in His counsels concerning the children of men, bringing to nought their vain endeavours, to fulfil his own purpose, when and how He will ! The next day, Andrew went away cursing the Monastery with a great curse, because there he had left his Master, and desiring that the whole valley might be swallowed up with all that dwelt in it. Those who heard the prophecy of the holy man were not a little disturbed and in wonder, when they saw him depart after such a manner. But God did not give a long trial to their weakness of faith.

Andrew for that day resisted victoriously the grace of God, but on the following night he was vanquished, and as it were made prisoner, by the Spirit of God, drawing him, and doing violence to him, so that he could not wait for day, but rising before the dawn, he came quickly like another

Saul, or rather like Saul changed into Paul, and gave himself up to the guidance of the holy Father.

The Blessed Henry, now clothed in the sacred habit, made much advance daily in all holy conversation. He was not however long allowed to lead the solitary life he had chosen. He was elected Bishop of Beauvais. As, however, it was well known that he would refuse to be Bishop, letters were written beforehand to Pope Eugenius, and Pope Eugenius wrote to the most' Blessed Bernard that he should be compelled to undertake the office of Bishop. Henry, thus besieged, had no road left him but to obey. Peter, Abbot of Cluny, was one of those who had conspired to make him accept the Bishopric. The Blessed Henry thus wrote to the Venerable Peter, "May God Almighty spare you, what is it that you have done? A man that was buried you have called again amongst men. It is through your counsel too much relied on that I am exposed to a sea of cares, and the depths of honours are again ready to swallow me up. I knew not, my mind troubled me for the chariots of Aminadab, which I who have need rather to be guided, have undertaken to guide. They have destined my hands to mighty things, I have need of strength. I am made a watchman of the house of Israel, I have need of prudence. I am become a debtor to the wise and to the unwise, I have need of justice. I am given as a preacher to the people of God, I have need of temperance, lest haply, when I have preached to others, I myself should be a castaway, which God forbid. But where are all these things, or who am I? O God of my life, Thine eyes have seen my imperfect being. O Lord, I have suffered violence, answer Thou for me, because obedience alone has forced me, without which, though a man seem faithful he is proved unfaithful. And as no one uses so great boldness as he, who sincerely loves, so as to a portion of my own soul, I bring to you this complaint. Why is it that by your letters to my Lord Abbot you have made my folly to be set up on a candlestick? You believed, and therefore you spoke. You neither desired to deceive or be deceived, but you have not escaped the latter thing."

Such murmurs did humility teach the Blessed Henry to make against the imposed office. In the exercise of his office he found many adversaries; even his own brother King Louis turned against him. He was slandered at Rome, and was turning his steps thither to defend himself when the holy Father Bernard with wiser counsel advised him to remain at home, himself writing a defence which was amply sufficient. Henry was raised after fourteen years to the Archbishopric of Rheims, A.D. 1163. He was called to his reward A.D. 1177.

LIFE OF BLESSED HERMAN,

ABBOT OF HEMMENRODE.

AT the time when the Cistercian Religion was
sending forth its first branches in all places,
there lived a certain man named Herman, one
highly respected for his goodness.   Born of noble
parents, who were themselves devoted to works of
piety, the youth was delivered by them to the care
of masters of excellent character, that he might both
be carefully educated in letters, and at the same
time imbued with sound morals.   He made quick
progress in learning, and having come to man's
estate, was made Canon of the Church of Bonne.
It was then that the mind of the pious young man
began to be illuminated with the light of heavenly
things, so that despising the things of this present
time, he conceived the desire of retiring to some
solitude, that making warfare under the banner of
the eternal King, he might one day secure for
himself eternal rest.

Bidding farewell to the world, he enrolled himself as a Novice in the Monastery of Hemmenrode.
His whole care was how he might please God, and
deliver himself wholly to the divine service.
Thirsting after God alone, and the heavenly country, by constant contemplation of the things above,

he set no value on the trifling goods of this earth,
so that, if the whole world had been made over
into his hands he would have refused the gift as
of no value. The Father of mercies who knew
the purity of his heart, and the trueness of his
love, adorned the soul of His beloved one with
many gifts.

When he had entered on the state of the priesthood, and approached in fear and trembling to
sacrifice the Lamb without spot, he experienced
such sweetness of spiritual delights as could be
expressed by no word of the tongue. On a certain day, in the choir of the Convert Brothers, as
he celebrated the Mass at the altar of S. John
Baptist, whilst with great devotion he was reading
the sacred Canon, a certain Convert Brother named
Henry saw a dove of marvellous whiteness sitting
near the chalice. There appeared also in the
hands of the Blessed Herman a very beautiful
Infant, who seemed to leave his hands and ascend
to the top of the cross, then again descending was
received by the priest under the species of bread.
The Brother knew all these things by revelation,
for Blessed Herman saw nothing with the eyes of
his body, only that his soul perceived within the
sweetness of heavenly grace. And this perhaps
was the reason why the vision was not shown him,
that not seeing yet still believing, he might merit
the more. For as S. Gregory says in his twenty-
sixth homily on the gospel :—" That has no merit
of which human reason affords the proof."

The fore-mentioned Henry told the Blessed Herman sometimes, how frequently he saw the demons going about the Choir, but principally during the hours of the night. Herman was inflamed with the desire of the same gift, and earnestly besought God to grant him this grace, and his petition was presently granted. There came soon after the Feast of S. Martin, and during the Matins he saw a demon in form of a square built rustic enter the presbytery at the lower end. His chest was broad, shoulders sharp, neck short, his hair shaven away from the forehead, and the rest hanging down like beards of corn. He came up to a certain novice and stood before him; just then the Blessed Herman turned his eyes away from him, and when he sought again to see him, he had disappeared.

On S. Cunibert's night, when he was standing in the Abbot's choir, he saw two demons enter by the presbytery, and come up by little and little to the Abbot's stall between the Choir of the Monks and Novices. When they had come to the corner where the two walls join each other, there leaped forth a third demon, who associating himself to them, went out with them. They went so close to him as they passed, that he could have touched them with his hand. As he watched them diligently, he observed that they did not touch the ground with their feet, being indeed powers of the air. One of the two first had the countenance of a woman, having a black veil on her head, and her person enveloped in a black cloak. The Monk, near whom the third demon had been resting, was one of an evil tongue, and not a little slothful, often sleeping in Choir, and not willing at the psalmody, more ready to eat and drink, than to sing.

When on a certain night the Invitator of the week had begun the Antiphon, and the Monk next him had intoned the psalm at a moderate pitch of voice, Herenwick, the Prior, with the other an-cients, carried on the psalm at the same pitch. But a silly youth, at the lower end of the Choir, displeased at the psalm being begun on so low a note, raised it as much as five whole tones, and the superior not giving way to him, he refused to yield, and with much pertinacity bore off the vic-tory. In the next verse, some in the opposite Choir helped him, and so the rest, on account of the scandal, and for fear of discord, sang not at all. But the Blessed Herman saw a demon in the form of a red hot piece of iron, leaping forth from the triumphant Monk, and transferring himself to that Monk in the opposite Choir, who had given the help to strengthen his side. From this it is collected, that a low chant, with devotion of heart, is more pleasing to God than voices proudly raised up to heaven.

Another night, having got to his place in Choir at the Vigils before the Brethren were come in, he directed his eyes to the window that he might admire the clearness of the heavens, when suddenly there met his gaze a very black and gigantic demon, who ascending to him through the upper Choir, passed him and went out. Another time, having moved from his stall in order to admonish the Brethren, he saw a horrible looking demon rush in between the Abbot's and Prior's stall, and seeing that no entrance could be effected there, because the Abbot stood in the way, he hastily passed into the Choir of the Novices, and there joined himself to an old Monk, one of no good manners, but slothful and a murmurer. Herman often saw these demons in one form or other, and was at last so afflicted with the sight of them, that he prayed the Lord, whilst saying a Mass of the Holy Ghost, that He would graciously be pleased to free him from these visions, and after that time he saw them but seldom, and not in the same clear manner.

The Abbot of Hemmenrode seeing in the holy man so many virtues, and that he was a living exemplar of Monastic perfection, chose him for his Prior, that with the help of such a man he might more easily sustain the burden of the Monastery. Then the Blessed Herman, inflamed with the zeal of Religion, began to watch over the flock of the Lord, as one who should render account both to the chief pastor of souls, and to his Abbot. Those whom he found wanting in fervour he, with pious works rather than sharp words, incited to desires of perfection. Those who were already well inclined to virtue he, with honeyed words, confirmed in their purpose ; and many whom the storm of temptation had almost overset, he delivered by his powerful counsel from the nets of the evil one.

A certain Novice, having quietly passed his year of probation, and expressed his desire in Chapter to receive the tonsure of a Monk when the Brother who should shave him came for him, refused to receive the tonsure, being so overcome with fear, that his cheeks became pale, and his whole body trembled. Herman, seeing that it was a temptation of the most Wicked One, came up to the Novice, and with an air of pleasantry, caught him in his arms, and embracing him, pressed him to his heart. Immediately the temptation of the Evil One left him, and with a gladsome countenance he allowed himself to be shaved, the embrace of the holy man having calmed all the terrible tempest excited by the Enemy.

Now the brightness of the holy conversation of the Blessed Herman daily increased ; wherefore as Aaron was called by the Lord to the priesthood, so Herman was raised by the Lord to the dignity of Abbot, and this He signified to him before in a vision, in which he beheld the cross given him as is the custom, on leaving a Monastery to found a fresh Religious House. He went forth, therefore, from Hemmenrode in the year 1134, to Mount Stromberg, and there endured great labours and hardships, which however he bore cheerfully for His sake, Who being rich took upon Him the form of a servant and became poor and needy.

17

At length, seeing the difficulties that his children were oppressed by, he removed in the fourth year to the valley of S. Peter, where he laid the foundation of the Monastery of Heisterbach, which he enlarged much in after time, God protecting him and directing his work. The strict Religious Observance of the holy Abbot and his Monks began to pour its light like the rising sun over a country covered with the thick darkness of sin. Many of high rank, both clerks and laity, fled for refuge to this asylum, throwing off the miserable slavery of their vices. Some became members of their Community, others by their counsel and prayer were directed in such sort that they freed themselves from the chains of their besetting sins.

Meanwhile, the Monks of Hemmenrode having to elect a new Abbot by the divine inspiration fixed upon Herman, and so he was restored to the Monastery, of which he had formerly been Prior. Leaving, therefore, his Monks at Heisterbach in great sorrow for his departure, he returned to Hemmenrode with all humility, remembering that sentence, " in proportion as thou art greater, so humble thyself in all things." He was to his disciples like a servant rather than a master, showing, however, in his own person, a pattern of all perfection of modesty and discipline. When singing in Choir, he did so with rapt attention and reverence of body, diligently meditating in his heart the words that came forth from his lips. This he impressed with frequent exhortation of his Monks, especially to be attentive at the matin prayers. When, therefore, on a certain feast-day, he went round as was his custom, whilst the *Te Deum* was being sung, to stir up the Brethren, he turned into the Choir of the Convert Brothers, from the altar there flew a snow-white dove, which settled on the head of Herman, and remained there till he went out of the Choir; then it returned to the cross upon the Altar. This Henry, the Convert Brother, saw oftentimes to occur, and when the Abbot began the reading of the Gospel after the finishing of the *Te Deum*, the same bird used to fly to a column near the desk, and sitting there seemed to listen to the divine word. When the reading was ended it returned to the cross. The Blessed Henry often beheld this marvellous thing, by which the great purity of Herman was manifested, and with what ardour he was inflamed by the same Spirit of love.

A certain Canon of S. Mary's at Cologne, bidding farewell to the world, took the habit of Religion at Hemmenrode. His brothers, who were soldiers, and men of rank in the world, hearing of his conversion, came to the Monastery, and with many words persuaded him to return to the world. They laid before him the austerity of the Order, and the fact that he was in debt. "It was but reasonable he should return," they said, "to the world, in order to be able to pay his debts, and then go to the Monastery to serve the Lord without scruple."

The miserable man was led away by their speeches, gave his consent, and fell into the snare of the devil. Herman, seeing it, groaned within himself, and turning to the soldiers, he said, with much sorrow of heart, "This day you have cast your brother out of paradise, and laid him in hell." They, however, despising his words, led their brother away. He returned to his prebend, and far from paying his debts, gave himself up to a loose disorderly life. After a few years he fell grievously ill, and being spoken to of making his Confession and receiving the Holy Communion, he lent a deaf ear to all that was said. From this he fell into a delirium, and called frequently by their names the wretched beings with whom he had been in the habit of sinning, thus coming to a miserable end, and justifying the words of the holy Father which he had despised.

It may be worth while here to relate the terrible vision and conversion of a certain Abbot of Morimond, which Herman was often wont to tell the Brethren of, that he might render them more cautious against the snares of the devil. Herman had seen this Abbot, heard him speak, and had beheld his actions as those of one who had once been dead, and had risen again.

This Abbot, when a young man, studied at the University of Paris with other scholars. Being of a dull disposition, and a slippery memory, he could scarce learn or remember anything; so that he was looked upon as a half-idiot by many, upon which he was much disturbed in mind. It happened one day when he was ill, that Satan appeared to him and said, "If you will only worship me, I will give you the knowledge of all kinds of learning." Hearing this, the young man was amazed, and replied to the tempter, "Get behind me, Satan, for thou shalt never be my lord, nor I thy servant." And as he consented not, the devil, violently opening his hand, placed in it a stone, and said, "As long as you keep this stone in your hands, you shall know all things."

When the Enemy was gone, the student rose, entered the schools, proposed questions, and so disputed as to carry off the victory. All were astonished at the eloquence of him, whom they had considered to be almost an idiot. He however held his peace, and told no one the secret of his newly acquired knowledge. But falling dangerously ill, he called for a priest, and among other things mentioned how he had received the stone from the devil, and with it the gift of knowledge. The priest answered him, "Foolish man! cast away from thee the cleverness of the devil, lest thou be found a stranger to the knowledge of God." He being very frightened cast away the stone, and with it lost his deceitful knowledge. The cleric then died ; his body was carried to the Church, and the scholars ranging themselves round the bier, sang psalms in a Christian manner. Meantime the devils bore off his soul to a terribly deep valley, out of which there poured forth a

sulphurous smoke. The devils ranged themselves
on each side of the valley, and as it were playing
at ball, they cast the wretched soul one to another,
and it seemed as if they received it after flying
through the air into their claws, which sharply
pierced into its substance, causing unutterable pain.

Whilst this was going on, the Lord in mercy
sent some heavenly personage, one very reverent to
behold, who gave this message to the demons:
"Hear you," said he, "the Lord most high has
commanded that you let go that soul who has been
deceived by you." They at once released the soul,
which fled back and returned to reanimate its lifeless body. The cleric, thus returning to life, rose
from the bier, and the scholars in great fear took
to flight. He immediately entered the Cistercian
Order, and he chastised his body with such rigour,
that it was plain to all that he had suffered the
pains of Purgatory.

These things, as we have before said, Herman
used to relate, and when Cæsar of blessed memory
asked him if he had ever seen him laugh, he
answered, "Know that he was of such a gravity
in all his behaviour that I never saw in him any
sign of levity. Never did I see him even smile,
or give utterance to any light word." The cleric
said that when carried to Purgatory, his soul was
as it were like a globe of glass, with eyes behind
and before, and full of knowledge. He made
known also to the scholars seated round the bier,
what they had been doing. "You," he said,

"were playing at dice; and you, (he said to others,) were saying the psalter with all diligence." We ought therefore to be glad that a man, who being stripped of the body, had heard and seen such things, passing by other Orders entered the Cistercian, in which he became afterwards Abbot of Morimond.

There was at Hemmenrode a certain Convert Brother, a very good man, and of regular life. He was Master of the Grange of that house. Another simple Convert Brother used frequently to see near him, when occupied either in labour of the hands or in other business of the house, an Angel of the Lord accompanying him. He related this to Blessed Herman, whereupon the holy man said to him, "Because you have mentioned this vision, you shall never see the angel any more." And so it came to pass; for though it does not appear to be a fault to have manifested the matter to his spiritual Superior, yet doubtless the Abbot detected somewhat of vain-glory, on account of the thing divinely revealed to him, for which fault he denoted this punishment.

At this time a noble lady, Alice of Molsberg, Countess of Freimberch, with the consent of her husband, Everard Burgrave, gave to the Abbot Henry certain farms to found a new Abbey of our Order. The house being finished was called Mary's Place, and Herman was appointed Abbot of it. The Countess died some time after, and as foundress her body was buried in the Monastery,

Whilst the body was lying on the bier, the Blessed Herman saw the Devil making the circuit of the bier and searching all its corners, as if he had lost something that had belonged to him. The Blessed man, without fear, offered up the sacrifice of his prayers for the soul of the pious woman.

Then certain relations of the noble Countess, she being now dead, began to harass with threats and violence the Monks of the Abbey she had founded, wishing to deprive them of their land. The Holy Mother of God, however, so defended them by her prayers to her Son, that the chief of all, Henry de Molsberg, was attacked in his own castle by a superior force and cast out from thence. Another great gentleman was killed by his own servant, and a third burst asunder whilst he was on his way to lay waste the Monastery. Another of the heirs hearing of these judgments came with fear and trembling to the Monastery, and said to Blessed Mary, "I renounce my share, holy Mary, keep what is thine for thyself."

The persecutions against the Abbey having brought down on these wicked men the judgments of God, the Abbot was allowed to possess his Monastery in peace. After giving to all a pattern of virtues together with the spirit of prophecy, and the revelation of secret things, he at length gave up his soul to Almighty God. His virtues and revelations are recounted in the Dialogues of Cæsar of Heisterbach.

LIFE OF THE VENERABLE FATHER
LOUIS OF ESTRADA,

ABBOT OF HORTE.

THE venerable Father Louis, a man of no mean abilities, having long had a good report amongst men, and especially amongst the Brethren of the Abbey of Horte, whither he had fled, leaving the world, was at length by the unanimous voice of the Brethren chosen Abbot.

His kindness and charity towards the poor of Christ was exceeding great. One day, whilst waiting in the Porter's lodge, he saw a poor man approaching, who had scarce enough clothing on him wherewith decently to cover his half-naked body. Entering quickly the chamber hard by, the holy Abbot put off his inner robe, and coming forth gave it to the poor man to cover his nakedness, not considering the danger he might run of himself catching some severe illness through the cold, to which he thus subjected himself, being now an old man, and subject to many infirmities.

In his days there was a great famine through all the land, and the poor came in great numbers, from all parts round about, to be fed at the gates of the Monastery. Indeed they built little huts and cabins in its neighbourhood, unable to procure food elsewhere. The holy Abbot gave God great thanks for thus giving him an opportunity of ministering to the wants of His people, glad that the Almighty should use him as an instrument for conveying so great a benefit. He and the Monks were of one heart and soul on the matter, and even spared a part of their frugal repast, to add to what might be given to the famishing. Every day after dinner they came forth to wait upon the poor.

As the summer advanced, corn was hardly to be procured even at a very high price, and it seemed almost as if this whole multitude must perish for lack of bread. The Abbot, putting all his trust in God, poured forth his prayers before the Most High, and God lent a gracious ear to his supplications. Whilst the corn was yet green in all the surrounding country, it being still two months before the general time of harvest, the wheat on the Abbey lands was full ripe. This wonder God had wrought for the consolation of His servant, and lest so vast a multitude should perish of hunger.

Now during this famine, on the Thursday before Easter, a very great multitude had gathered together from all parts, because it was the custom of the Monastery to give a loaf of bread to all who came, besides other food. There had come there also the Duke of Medina to celebrate the Paschal season. He, beholding this vast multitude of people, and seeing that they had no means of sustenance, was filled with astonishment, not knowing how they could be supplied with necessary food. He asked the Abbot therefore if he intended to attempt to feed so great a multitude. The holy man replied that he would certainly do so. " I," answered the Duke, " could not do it without borrowing upon my estate." The Abbot replied that not only should he be able to supply them all with food, but even many more, if they came, such confidence he had in God. " But I should like to know," said the Duke, " what you will give them for food." The Abbot therefore brought him to the place, where the loaves were stored for distribution to the poor, telling him that each should have a loaf, and that there would be some over. This seemed incredible, for there were scarce two hundred loaves. The Duke, therefore, hardly believing it, asked the Abbot if he would allow his Steward, who had accompanied him to the Abbey, to be present when the distribution was made, that he might remark if any loaves were brought from any other place. This the Abbot willingly granted. The Steward therefore himself presided over the distribution of the loaves that day, giving them to other of the Duke's own servants, from the place where they were stored up, and the servants distributing them with their own hands to the people. They found not only enough, but even abundance to spare, after each one had received a loaf. This was the case not only with the bread but with the other provisions, which had been distributed. The servants, therefore, seeing this evident miracle, came and told to their Master all that had happened. The Duke then went to behold with his own eyes the loaves which were left, and seeing them, gave praise to God for the wonders He wrought by the hand of His servant. The Abbot, however, chid him for his want of faith.

Now, after the famine was over, one of the Monks was taken with a grievous fever, so that he despaired of life. The physician having given him up, the holy Abbot was told of it, and with sad mind went to visit the dying man. On his way, however, he besought the Lord that, if it might be, the poor Brother might be healed of his sickness. As the Abbot entered the door of the sick man's chamber, the Brother felt himself completely cured; so that, when the Abbot asked him with a gracious look how he did, he who had been given over to death replied that he now felt quite well, and that all his sickness was gone. The Brethren could not doubt that, by the merits and prayers of their holy Abbot, the sick man had been so suddenly restored to health, that he at once left his bed. For so wrapt in prayer was the man of God at times, that his countenance appeared shining with a heavenly light, and Angels were seen in his company.

The Blessed Abbot showed great zeal in the search for the bodies of S. Martin and S. Roderic, which had lain a long time neglected in the Church of Horte. Who can unfold the joy of the Brethren,

when the bodies of these two Saints were discovered, both of them uncorrupted. The body of
S. Martin emitted so sweet an odour, that it filled
not only the Church, but penetrated the Monastery, so that those who perceived it came hastening to the Church. There, with tears of devotion
and joy, they kissed the feet of their father, beholding the evident miracle of his wonderful pre-
servation. The head, however, of S. Martin was
not with the body, it having been carried to the
Church of Sagunt, of which he had been Bishop,
by an Angel, in the form and appearance of a
young man.

The bodies, having remained some days in the
Choir, were carried in solemn procession, and then
placed with great pomp in a splendid shrine, at
the left of the high Altar. The Blessed Louis
only reserved a few shreds of the vestments of S.
Martin, and a little of the skin rubbed from his
feet. These he always had present when he received the vows of Novices.

When his end was nigh he had the relics of S.
Martin brought to him, and, frequently kissing
them, invoked his aid, to whose presence he hoped
shortly to be united. The Monks stood around,
weeping, and bewailing the loss of so great a
Father, and thus he went to his reward on the
second of June, 1581. His body was buried in an
honourable place near the Presbytery Step.

LIFE OF THE BLESSED ALEYS,

NUN OF S. MARY'S CHAMBER.

THE Blessed Aleys was a child of good promise from her earliest years, and being a lover of solitude, entered the Nunnery of the Chamber of Mary.

The graciousness of her demeanour was such that all loved her, for she compassionated their miseries, endured their weaknesses, was kind, social, and peaceful. Knowing that idleness is the enemy of the soul, she was diligent at work, never neglecting anything.

Once, when quite a little girl, she let fall a candle from the lantern she held, which was at once extinguished, but when she had found it on the pavement, and had taken it up again, by a marvel of God's right hand it was rekindled into a flame.

A certain lady coming one night to the Church, and seeing it as it were all in flames, looked within, and saw the handmaid of God, from whose person a bright light issued on all sides, like the glory of God.

On the Feast of Easter, while the Response was being sung, *The Lord is risen from the tomb,* the Blessed Aleys, looking up, saw heaven as it might be a sepulchre opened, and a bright glory coming forth like fire towards the Monastery. A Sister who was with her at her side saw it also, and cried out, but the Blessed Aleys put her finger to her lips as a sign to her to be silent.

Being deprived by the disease of leprosy of the use of her left eye, she offered this affliction to God in behalf of the King of the French against the infidels at Jerusalem.

On S. Barnabas' Eve, she was anointed with the holy oil. A Nun sitting by her side, said to her by way of solace, " This day the Son of God was betrayed for our redemption to the Jews, and scourged, and condemned to the death of the Cross." At these words, inflamed with the desire of heaven, the Blessed maid replied, " Tomorrow, at dawn of day, I shall depart from this world." It fell out as she had said, it being the year of our Lord 1250, on the eleventh of June.

She appeared in great glory to a sister of hers, who lived in a village not far from the Monastery on that same night, and miracles were wrought by her relics.

LIFE OF SAINT LUTGARD,

CISTERCIAN NUN.

THE Blessed Lutgard was born in Brabant, in the year of grace 1182, of noble parents. They lived at Tongres. Her father, a man of the world, imbued the mind of the young girl with a love of the passing vanities of time, and up to the age of twelve she gave her heart a good deal to these things. Her mother, however, was of a wholly different spirit, and did what she could to draw the mind of her daughter towards the things of another world. Thus influenced, she began to change her thoughts by the operation of grace, and in the year of Redemption 1194, she entered a Monastery of the Order of S. Benedict, near to Saint Catherine in the diocese of Liege.

The discipline of Monasteries in that age was very relaxed, for a certain young man came thither to seek her, desiring to obtain her consent to marry him. This foolish young girl, taking pleasure in these attentions, freely allowed the young man to converse with her in speeches of love. As she was listening to his addresses, there appeared by his side another Lover, who, jealous of her affections, showed to her His pierced Side, and said to her, "Here cast your eyes that you may

know what you ought to love, and why you ought
to love. Here you will find delights that will fill
your heart with sweetest consolations. Reject,
then, with horror, the caresses of this foolish
love."

This vision so changed in an instant the heart
of the young Lutgard, as to dissipate all the mists
of the vanities of this world, and attach her solely
to the love of Jesus Christ.

Now as the Monastery was not strictly enclosed,
at the request of one of her sisters, she went out
of her Monastery to visit her. A young man,
hearing of her intended visit, waylaid her on the
road, with a number of his companions, and it
was all she could do to save herself from his violence by flight.

The Blessed Lutgard now determined no longer
to trifle with the graces she had received, but to
give herself wholly to the divine Spouse. Her retired life was now such as to excite the remarks of
the more careless of her Sisters, who looked upon
it as a passing fervour, of which she would soon
tire. They ridiculed her for her strictness, but
Our Lord Jesus Christ appeared to her with Saint
Catherine, to whom she had had recourse in this
trial, and strengthened her to endure with courage
all the trials she might meet with. The Lord,
however, showed visibly His favours to her, even
in the sight of all her sisters, for when, on the
Feast of Pentecost, she sang the "Veni Creator,"

18

she was seen by them lifted up above the ground about two feet.

In her prayer her love made her to converse with Jesus Christ in great familiarity, and when she was forced to attend to some exterior employment, she would say simply to Him, " Wait for me, please, here, my Lord Jesus, I shall be back again to see you, as soon as I have finished."

When she was in the Monastery of Vuyere, there was a Nun there, called Elizabeth, who was afflicted with a sickness that obliged her to eat almost every hour of the day. The Blessed Lutgard, after having one day been to communion, was conversing with Jesus Christ in an unspeakable delight of heart, when she suddenly remembered the sick Nun; then turning to our Lord, she said to Him, " I have not opportunity any longer now to stay conversing with Thee; go to Sister Elizabeth, who is so sick, and fill her heart with Thy delights, and meanwhile permit me to take a little refreshment." At these words Jesus Christ left her, and went to fill Sister Elizabeth with His consolations, and delivered her from the troublesome necessity of eating at every hour. This Nun who, up to this time, could not rise from her bed, was after this able to follow the regular exercises of the Community.

The Blessed Lutgard, having learned that a great friend of' hers, the Abbot Simon, of the Cistercian Order, was dead, undertook great penances for the deliverance of his soul. As she spared nothing to gain this favour, Jesus Christ appeared to her, and told her He would soon do mercy to him, for whom she prayed. The Blessed Lutgard, not contented with the answer, pressed yet more urgently upon Him, and said, " All that you would otherwise give to me, give to this suffering soul, for I will not cease to shed tears, nor will I take any consolation till his soul is delivered." Then the Lord, wearied out by her importunity, appeared to her, showing her the soul of the Abbot, delivered from his pains, and said to her, " Rejoice, My spouse, behold the soul of him for whom you prayed." Hearing this, the holy Nun prostrated in great gladness of heart and humble thanksgiving, and the soul of the Abbot, thanking the holy maiden, was received up with great glory into heaven.

God being so gracious to her in the granting of her requests, the holy maid besought Him also in behalf of all for whom her kind heart felt deeply. The Lord gave her the grace of healing sicknesses, but this drawing such a number of persons to seek her help, and destroying her quiet and her prayer, she besought the Lord to exchange it for some better gift. Our Lord asked her what gift she would desire, on which she asked for the gift of understanding the mysteries of the psalms, that she might recite them with greater devotion. However, reconsidering her request, and thinking she might obtain something more advantageous to her, she begged instead that our Lord would give her His Heart. Our Lord, answering her, said, "But I would have yours also," to which the holy maiden gladly consented, and from that day forth, this mystery took place in her, for instead of her own heart there seemed to be within her the heart of Jesus Christ. Never after that did any bad thought seem to have the power of entering at all within her.

Our Lord was so pleased with this holy maid for having preferred the possession of His Heart to every other thing, that He gave her also the knowledge of the mysteries of the Scriptures, which she had been willing to forego in order to obtain the gift of His Divine Heart; and she had so deep and piercing an understanding of the things of God as to astonish those who were made aware of it with the greatest amazement. And, though she did not know the Latin tongue, she had given to her to know the sense of the prayers, and other things she recited in the Office.

Once on a time, when very sick, and all bathed in a cold sweat, which broke out at every pore, she thought to absent herself from the Vigils of the night, thinking her health required it, when she heard a voice, saying, "Why are you lying in your bed in this way? Rise at once and do penance for sinners, and think not of your bodily health." At this voice she at once rose in great fear, and as she entered the Church, our Lord appeared to her, fastened to the cross, and all covered with blood. Unfastening one of His arms from the cross, He embraced with it the holy maid, so that her mouth was drawn close to His sacred Side.

The Blessed Lutgard was now twenty-four years of age, when she was elected Prioress of her Convent. This employment was far from her liking, who had wished rather to sit at the feet of Jesus with Mary than to seek to govern others. She had for some time before had the desire to leave her Convent, which was in a relaxed state, for some stricter Monastery. Her election as Prioress made her the more urgent to execute this design, and she looked about to see where she might find a secure refuge. Her first idea was to seek some Cistercian Monastery, where Flemish was spoken, but God disposed it otherwise, for, asking the advice of a holy Nun, named Christina, and of a great Theologian, named John Lyran, they both gave counsel that she should retire into the Monastery of Vuyere in the diocese of Liege, where French alone was spoken, of which she understood nothing whatsoever. At first she could not think of such a thing without the greatest repugnance. But Jesus Christ told her by a secret voice that, unless she followed this counsel, He would withdraw from her. At the same time Saint Christina, coming to find her, said to her, "For me, I would rather be in hell with God, than be in heaven with the Angels, but without God."

Unable longer to resist, the Prioress, without taking any leave of her Nuns, for fear their affectionate tears might destroy her resolution, went off to the Monastery of Vuyere, having been twelve years at that of Saint Catherine, and a few months in the office of Prioress. She prayed, however, for the Nuns she left behind, and the holy Virgin, appearing to her, assured her that the blessing of God should be upon the Monastery, which effectually took place.

Not a long time after the Blessed Lutgard had entered her new home, she was tried with great temptations, not knowing if in this she had really done the will of God or merely followed the bent of her own mind. She supplicated our Lord to give her some distinct token of His Holy Will in this matter, and, whilst she was praying, she heard a voice uttering the words, "Fear not, the life you have embraced is agreeable to God." This assurance, however, did not last long, and being again in great alarm, our Lord was pleased by a yet more evident sign to signify His good pleasure. For, whilst the Nuns were holding their Conference, there appeared in the midst of them a man venerable to behold, who, saluting Lutgard in the midst of her Sisters, said to her, in the hearing of them all, "The Most High wishes to assure you for the future that He is well pleased in you."

Being delivered now from all disquietudes, the Blessed Lutgard gave herself up to a life of pure prayer. Her principal petition was, however, that God would be pleased shortly to remove her from this perishable life, and translate her to endless bliss in the true heavenly country. One day, when she was thus pouring out her soul before God, the Lord Christ appeared to her, showing to her the wounds of His hands, feet, and side. As He showed them, He said, "Listen to the cries which My wounds make to resound in your ears, that I may not have shed My Blood in vain." She said to Him, "What cry is it, Lord Jesus Christ?" He answered, "a cry . to appease the wrath of My Father against sinners by tears and penance, lest He should bring them to destruction." By this answer, the Lord make known to her that she should not cease to pray for the conversion of sinners, and to obtain pardon for their iniquities. In this she now continually employed her time. She never was able to learn the French tongue. This she obtained by the intercession of our Blessed Lady, lest, being made Abbess of some Monastery, she should be hindered in her work of prayer. Her fame being spread abroad, many Monasteries would have chosen her to this Office but for this hindrance.

Whilst occupied in this holy work of prayer, the holy Virgin appeared to her one day, with a countenance sad and pale. Lutgard, in sorrow, asked her the cause. The holy Virgin replied, "Heretics and false Christians have covered the face of my Son with vile spittle, and they have crucified Him afresh. Weep and sigh and fast for seven years, lest the wrath of God destroy the world." The Blessed Lutgard therefore continued for seven years to fast on bread with a small quantity of beer. Her superiors wished her to add a few legumes, but though she tried to obey she was not able to do it. Nevertheless her natural force did not abate, but she was strong both in mind and body.

Scarcely was this fast over, when our Lord appeared to her covered with wounds, offering Himself to His Father to obtain grace for sinners, and turning to her, He said, " You see how I offer Myself entirely to the Father for the conversion of sinners. It is thus I desire that you offer yourself entirely to Me to turn from them My anger, which is ready to consume them." He then ordered her another fast of seven years, and this order He repeated to her several times. It was revealed to Saint Mary of Oignies that no one prayed so effectually for sinners and for the souls in Purgatory as the Blessed Lutgard.

The holy Mother was made by the General of the Dominican Friars the protector of all his Order, such confidence had he in the efficacy of her prayers. The Lord gave to her all kinds of miraculous graces, such as to see the secrets of the heart, and to deliver souls from divers temptations. Sometimes she appeared to persons in their sleep, and delivered them from temptations, by which they were tried.

There was a Cistercian Nun so troubled, to whom she appeared, telling her she should be delivered from her temptations. This Nun, after

some years, came to Vuyere, and without ever
having seen her, except in a dream, knew her at
once from her appearance. As the Blessed Lutgard had delivered her from her temptations, she
besought her to obtain for her the strength to be
able to abstain from flesh-meat, and so to endure
the penances of the Order. The Blessed Mother,
being thus pressed, promised not only to obtain
for her to be able to abstain from flesh-meat, and
to have health enough to endure the austerities of
the Order, but also to do other mortifications to
which God inspired her. From that day forth
this Nun had such a disgust of flesh-meat, that
she never tasted it any more; her health was quite
restored, and she could endure all the penances of
which promise had been given.

Now although the Blessed Lutgard was unable
to speak the French tongue, yet the Almighty
God suffered this not to be a hindrance to her
being plainly understood, and to her understanding of others, when charity so required. There
came once to the Monastery a woman, who was in
despair of her salvation. Others had tried, but in
vain, to instil hope into her heart. She was
counselled, therefore, to recommend herself to the
prayers of the handmaid of God. More it was
said could not be done, because she was a French
woman, only speaking her own language, nor understanding any other than her own. However,
the Blessed Lutgard, not content with merely
praying for her, sent for her, and they held a con-

versation together, one speaking Flemish, and the other French, yet understanding each other perfectly well. The woman was quite freed from her temptation, and remarked that although she had been told that the Blessed Lutgard knew nothing but Flemish, it was quite a mistake, for that she could speak French very well.

It was the custom of the Blessed Lutgard to go to Communion every Sunday. Now few persons used in those days to communicate so often. Some, therefore, thought that it ought not to be permitted, and the Abbess forbade her to do so. The handmaid of God submitted to this as to everything else, but she warned the Abbess that Jesus Christ would make His displeasure felt at such a prohibition. And so it was, for the Abbess was seized with such pains that she could not even go to the Church, and, these pains increasing, she thought best to remove the prohibition, when at once her pains ceased. Almighty God, that it might be known that it was pleasing to Him that she should communicate so often, caused that, when she was too weak to come up alone to the altar, two Angels should be seen visibly supporting her steps. At another time the holy Virgin and Saint John Baptist were seen accompanying her, as she went to and came back from Communion.

For eleven years before her death the Blessed Mother was deprived of the sight of her eyes. This affliction was received by her with joy, as shutting out from her view all the things of earth, so that she had no longer any visible objects to distract the eyes of her heart from fixing her gaze on the Divine Light. Our Lord also, to console her the more, revealed to her that on this account she should go straight from earth to heaven, without passing by the way of Purgatory.

The evil spirits were in such dread of the Blessed Lutgard, that they dared not to approach any place where she was praying. A sign of the cross from her put them at once to flight, or even a little verse of a psalm. This made her admire the wonderful force of the sacred words. One day, when a certain Nun was dying, the devil appeared to the Blessed Lutgard in an insulting manner. He told her how he had tormented the dying Nun, but that, when the Community had begun the accustomed prayers, he found himself powerless. Whilst on a day the holy Mother was at Office in Choir, another Nun saw a bright flaming light coming forth from her mouth, and rising up on high.

The Nuns who were in the Infirmary were careless in their manner of reciting Office. The Blessed Lutgard forewarned them that at her death the judgment of God would overtake them. When she died, a pestilence carried off fourteen Nuns in a very short while. The rest, in fear, corrected themselves, and the plague immediately ceased.

A short time after the Blessed Lutgard had, finished her second seven years' fast, she received an order from heaven to begin a third fast of seven years, to avert from the Church a dreadful calamity. It was after finishing this third fast that it pleased the Lord to call her to Himself. At the same time she had a vision, in which she beheld the soul of the Cardinal James Vitry carried up into heaven. In a transport of joy she asked him when it was that he died, not having known that he had passed into the next life. He answered that it was four days ago, during which time he had been in Purgatory. "But why," answered she, "did you not at once let me know you were in Purgatory, that our Sisters might have delivered you from your pains?"—"It was," he said, "because our Lord did not wish you to have the pain of knowing that I was there." He added, that she should soon follow him out of this life.

The Blessed handmaid of God, for her part, longed for this time, when she should put off the burden of the flesh, and be united for evermore to the Lord. About a year before her deliverance, Jesus Christ Himself appeared to her, and with a look full of tenderness, said, "I do not wish you to be separated from Me any more. I only ask this year for these three things: first, that you render Me continual thanks for the favours that I have done you, and for that purpose you ask the intercessions of the Saints. Secondly, that you pour yourself out entirely before the Father for the conversion of sinners. Thirdly, that you have no other care but to desire vehemently to enjoy My presence."

Again, towards Easter, about two months before her death, our Lord again appeared to her in great glory with His holy Mother. The Blessed Lutgard, complaining gently to Him of the length of her exile, he answered, "You shall not complain much longer of the pains of this life. I prepare for you a peace and rest that will never end, where you will find unspeakable refreshment and crowns that never fade, for I do not wish to be deprived of your presence any more."

Fifteen days before her departure the holy Virgin appeared to her with Saint John Baptist, and said to her, "Your end is now close at hand. The blessed citizens of heaven await you." Many other Saints appeared to her, and amongst them some of her own acquaintance who had gone before.

She still, however, to the last, prayed for sinners. One of her friends, who despaired of salvation, came to ask her prayers. She addressed prayers to God on her behalf, but not being readily heard, she said to Him, "Either pardon this sinner, or blot me out of the book of life." The Lord answered, "I pardon her, and I will pardon all that commend themselves to your prayers."

Three days before her death she fell into her mortal malady, and speaking to a Nun near her, she said, "The Monastery is filled with the heavenly host. The Saints and Blessed are here pre-

sent, and several of our Sisters." Then she remained in silence ravished in God, for the whole
day. The next day, which was a Saturday, being
the sixteenth of June, A.D. 1246, she received the
Sacraments of the Church. Then lifting her eyes
to heaven, she gave her soul up to the Lord amidst
the prayers of her Sisters, and the hymns of the
heavenly armies, who led forth this pure soul to
the throne of the Most High, to drink with them
of that river of delights which makes glad the city
of God.

Her face after death had the lustrous whiteness
of the lily. She appeared to divers persons in
great glory, and God rendered testimony to her
by many miracles wrought through her intercessions.

LIFE OF BLESSED ARNULPH,

MONK OF VILLERS.

THE Blessed Arnulph came of parents of moderate condition in life. He was born at Brussels in the duchy of Brabant. God who, for the working out of His unsearchable counsels, sometimes permits His elect to fall into the ways of sin, did so in the case of Arnulph. When he was a young man, he fell deep into the disorders of the flesh. A divine light fell upon him, revealing to him the shameful slavery in which he was sunk. The Lord touched his heart efficaciously, at the same time giving him grace to conceive a great horror of the foul sins he had so delighted in. Then waking, as it were, out of a deep sleep, he came forth from the sepulchre in which he had been so long buried, and hasted to be loosed from his bands through the salutary sacrament, which Christ has left in His Church for the setting free of the sinner. Through the grace of this sacrament, he obtained, as it were, the resurrection of his soul, and a new life ; and, bidding farewell for ever to his unhappy disorder, he began to live the life of the righteous. From that time forward he avoided sedulously the company of the worldly, joining himself to that of persons of good reputation, in order that, by their prayers and counsel, he might be better furthered in all his good endeavours.

On all Sundays and Festivals he assisted at the nightly Vigils, and if it happened that he was so oppressed with sleep as to arrive too late for the commencement of the Office, he felt so ashamed that, instead of entering the Church, he remained outside in a place where the water from the roof might drop upon him.

The Enemy, irritated that Arnulph had escaped out of his snare, roused up an impudent woman to tempt him to sin. The valiant soldier of Christ rejected the temptation with horror. Esteeming, however, that flight is a more prudent course in such matters, he determined to leave the world altogether, and for this end retired into the Monastery of Villers, in the diocese of Namur. Into this Monastery the Abbot Charles received him in the year of grace 1202, as a Convert Brother, he being then twenty-two years of age.

In the middle of his year of Noviciate, he had a strong temptation to leave the Monastery. The life seemed to him far too easy. " Why," said he to himself, " did I come here ? Was it to pass a useless life ? Had I remained in the world, I could have lived far more rigorously than I do here. I have here everything in plenty, both for food and for clothing. Nothing is wanting to me. I am therefore wasting my time. My days will pass away without fruit and without recompense."

Instead, however, of leaving, he invented some mortifications by which to afflict his body. He bound two cords of hair round his body so tight, that the pain of them sometimes made him ready to faint. This he did secretly, but it being discovered, his Father Master forbade him to do it, upon which he gave it up. He was permitted, however, by his Father Master to resume this penance, whereupon he made a cord more rough than before, which he allowed to remain so long bound round his body, that it pierced into his flesh, and his flesh began to corrupt and to breed worms. He then, with great pain, drew it off, lest the stench of his corrupted flesh should be disagreeable to the Brothers. It had stuck so fast, that the flesh came away with it.

In order to make up for the loss of his cord, he got permission to take the discipline. One of the Monks, hearing him at his task, counted more than a thousand blows. As he struck, the blood leaped out on all sides. One day, by the severity of his scourging, his whole body had become like one wound, but on the following day all was completely healed, a certain blackness alone remaining where the wounds had been the most severe.

This heavenly favour did not make him relax in his penance, but only stimulated him to fresh fervours. From his neck to his knees he covered his body with an iron cilice, very sharp pointed; his bed was made of some sticks, over which was laid a coverlet, and his pillow was a stone. His

19

food was black bread, such as is made for dogs, and some vegetables kept till they were beginning to corrupt. Amidst all this penance he still continued to labour with the rest of the Brethren. He did nothing without the permission of his superiors, who saw in his extraordinary way of life an evident inspiration of heaven. His Abbot, however, having one day sent him a better portion of food, he took it with thankfulness, and ate it.

The Blessed man had a great love of God's poor, and one day got permission from his Abbot to give away forty loaves of bread. Some of the Brethren, not knowing he had received permission, made a complaint to the Abbot, who forgot by a divine providence the permission he had given, and put the man of God to penance for the transgression, making him to stand at the gate of the Monastery for his fault.

The innocent criminal bore all without murmuring. The Lord also filled his heart with great delights, and the most glorious Virgin Mother of God came to visit him, with her Son in her arms, at which sight he was filled with transports of joy.

It chanced that when the holy man was residing on a farm belonging to Villers, named Sart, he was told to go with a servant of the Monastery to Villers, to carry corn thither, and to bring back bread for the Brethren on the farm. Having unloaded his wagon at the mill, he went with it to a

Grange, called the new Court, for two pigs, which the Abbot had given him permission to have killed to feed the poor. He had these animals put in sacks, and placed thus in the wagon. Now, as they drew nigh to the Monastery, and these beasts were making a great noise, he feared some of the Brethren might suspect they were to be given away, and might be inclined to murmur. He therefore turned to the animals and addressed them as follows : "Listen to me," he said, "if God does not will that I should give you away to the poor, then continue to make a noise ; but if it be the will of God that I should satisfy the hunger of the poor with your flesh, then, in the name of our Lord Jesus Christ, I command you to be silent." The animals became perfectly still in a moment. The Brother entered the Monastery, filled his sacks with bread, and, though they were thrown into the wagon, upon those in which the pigs were tied up, they made no more noise than if they had been dead. When, however, the wagon had got well away from the walls of the Monastery, the animals began to make the same noise as before.

The Countess of Champagne, seeing her lands pillaged by the Lord Erald of Ramem, had recourse to the man of God. He assured her that, if she would build a Convent for Cistercian Nuns, she should be freed from this oppression. She did so, and the event proved the truth of the holy man's promise.

A gentleman, named Giles Bertold, came one day to consult him concerning some difficulties he had with regard to building a Monastery. Before he began to speak, the man of God told him all that was in his mind, and bade him build without any regard to the obstacles. The gentleman did so, and the Monastery was called the Valley of Roses, being of the Cistercian Order.

The Blessed Arnulph, when the rest of the Brethren went to the Dormitory, to take the meridian sleep, used, instead of this, to give himself to prayer. For this fault he was proclaimed in the Chapter, and at once gave up his evil habit. Now the Arch enemy, not easily bearing this, appeared to him one day, when, at the time of the meridian sleep, he had obediently gone to lie down in the Dormitory, and mocking him, said, "What has become of you? Where is your former fervour of devotion, which once made you pass this time in acts of piety and prayer? How changed and slack you are become, serving the ease of the body in sloth! How ashamed you ought to be! Rise now, courageously, and apply yourself to watching and prayer." The man of God, seeing the artifice of the Enemy, treated him with contempt, answering, "Begone, wretch! to your confusion and torment I will sleep and take my rest." Upon this the devil vanished.

When Arnulph was near his end, a Monk, who had been a physician in the world, feeling his pulse, told him he would never recover. Upon this the Blessed man, raising himself, embraced him, and thanked him for giving him so good tidings. His joy, indeed, was such, that all his pains seemed at once gone, and such consolations did he receive, that to the end he spoke, as though he were not a wit sick. Just before he passed away, he rose and stood up, leaning on a Brother named Ralph. At the moment of death he sunk on his knees, and with three sighs breathed out his soul. He was aged forty-eight years, of which twenty-six had been spent in the Monastery.

He appeared after his death in great glory to several persons, and the fame of his sanctity going abroad, many miracles were wrought either by his relics or his intercession in France, Germany, and Italy. Pope Gregory IX. desired to canonize him, but the General Chapter of Citeaux opposed his doing so, and he yielded to their advice. His life was written four years after his death, and he is esteemed one of the greatest Saints of the Order.

PRINTED BY RICHARDSON AND SON, DERBY.

www.ingramcontent.com/pod-product-compliance
Lightning Source LLC
Chambersburg PA
CBHW060600030726
47498CB00005B/1476